"Don't you dare," Helen croaked

"Dare what?" Mike demanded in that same dizzying undertone. "Dare show you why Eve was created?"

She felt his hand on her hair, stroking it down to her shoulders, his fingertips exploring her neck, her ear. And wherever he touched, a new fire darted through her. She couldn't let it go on, she would be consumed.

"Leave me alone." It came out slurred and reluctant as she dragged herself away.

"Shall I leave you? Is that really what you want me to do, Helen Thornton?" Chilled, she watched his black, gigantic shadow move toward the car.

"When I first saw you," she called across to him, "it wasn't Adam I thought of. It was the devil."

Jessica Marchant, a retired English teacher, and her ex-diplomat husband, Peter, enjoy a wonderful life, traveling extensively. Her first book was drawn from one such journey across Europe. They have lived all over the world, but at present reside in Exeter in Devon.

Books by Jessica Marchant

HARLEQUIN PRESENTS
1145—JOURNEY OF DISCOVERY

THE SPICE OF LOVE
Jessica Marchant

Harlequin Books

TORONTO • NEW YORK • LONDON
AMSTERDAM • PARIS • SYDNEY • HAMBURG
STOCKHOLM • ATHENS • TOKYO • MILAN

Original hardcover edition published in 1990
by Mills & Boon Limited

ISBN 0-373-03137-8

Harlequin Romance first edition July 1991

For my parents, Mary and Jack Clinton,
with love and gratitude

THE SPICE OF LOVE

Printed in U.S.A.

CHAPTER ONE

THE boisterous wind and the ceaseless hiss of rain drowned all other noise. If the car made any sound as it crested the hill and dropped along the narrow road, Helen Thornton didn't hear it. She didn't see it either, wasn't aware of its existence until, powerful headlights cutting through the downpour, it passed her and drew to a halt a little ahead, engine still running.

A tall, rain-blurred figure sprang out, and opened the nearest rear passenger door. 'Come on. In you get.'

Helen stiffened at the commanding tone. 'I most certainly will not!'

Best not to think of the danger she might be in. The village of Linrother lay two miles back in the valley, her home a mile ahead up the hill. In this weather, even at three on a Saturday afternoon, the moor was deserted.

Well, she wasn't one of the red-haired Thorntons for nothing. She could give a good account of herself if she had to. 'Thank you,' she added, less vigorous but still frosty. 'I'm quite happy walking.'

'Sooner you than me.'

The rain was already shining on his dark hair. He pushed the hair back and flattened it to the top of his head, though wet masses of it escaped and stood up above his ears. 'Look, if you'll only get in, we'll——'

Sheet lightning flickered, and the thunder followed almost at once. Helen gasped at the shock of brightness and noise, but not only at that. The momentary glare had thrown the features of her unwanted companion into strange relief.

Where had she seen those dark eyes before? And the lean, high cheekbones, and the hollows beneath, and the long, sardonic mouth? The lightning had gone but the image of the face stayed with her, winged eyebrows flaring outwards to the temples, hair pointing up either side of the head...

That was it. He was exactly like the picture in her book of old Northumbrian legends, of the devil bargaining for souls. And where were you more likely to meet the devil than on the moors in a flash of lightning?

'This is silly.' With an effort, she dragged her mind back to everyday things. 'Hot tea, buttered scones, dry clothes, that's what I need against this... this whatever-it-is.'

She thought hard of the bright kitchen of Thornton Pele, a mile over the hill. They'd walked to Pele Farm for lunch with their neighbour Will Purvis, and Helen had elected to walk back across her beloved moors in spite of the threatening weather.

'I can cope with that, and with this too,' she silently assured herself. 'He won't get the better of a Thornton.'

'For goodness' sake, woman.' The man laid a hand on her arm. 'Will you——'

'Let go!' She shook him off, and doubled her fists in the pockets of her dripping Barbour. 'How dare you touch me?'

With a show of confidence, she turned again up the hill. She hoped he wouldn't notice how she was studying the tussocks of heather either side of the road for a get-away track. Then, a new voice froze her in mid-stride.

'Helen!'

'Mother?' Helen couldn't believe her ears.

Meg Thornton rose from the front passenger seat, scarf pulled forward against the beating rain. 'You're soaked, Mike's soaked, I'm about to be soaked.' Her voice was urgent, but blessedly everyday. 'Are you staying out here till we're all struck by lightning as well?'

'But what are you——?'

'Get in, girl, get in!'

To her mother's relief, Helen obeyed at once. The man closed her door, and leapt for the driving seat while she was still trying to gather her wits.

Listening to rain drumming against luxurious metal and glass, Helen struggled to put her questions into words. But they were too many. Before she could get her tongue round any of them, Meg had started.

'Look at you. Like you've just come out of the sea.'

'I won't melt.' Helen took off her soggy scarf and shook out her wet-dulled, red-gold hair. 'I thought Will was bringing you back in the Land Rover.'

'He's still tinkering with the starter, and Mike here—oh.' Meg remembered introductions. 'Helen, this is Mike Armstrong.'

'Hi.' The driver greeted her with an easy swing of his broad shoulders, then turned to put the car back in gear.

In the confined space, his damp jacket gave off a clean, mossy smell. The rain-washed light showed him solid, substantial, altogether different from the phantom of the lightning-flash.

'Sorry I frightened you,' he threw over his shoulder. 'I took it for granted you'd see your mother in the car.'

'You didn't frighten me.' Helen quickly and instinctively denied what she had felt on first meeting him. 'But I'm a bit mystified. Where on earth did you spring from?'

'Mike offered to help me rescue you,' Meg said, as if that explained everything. 'I told you this rain wouldn't hold off.'

'I really don't mind it,' Helen protested, but mechanically. Her mother would never understand the exhilaration of being out in a storm, and she had long given up trying to explain it. Besides, she had to admit she'd been glad enough to be taken out of this one. She moved on the deep-sprung seat, aware of the wet running off her into soft, expensive leather.

'I'm sorry about your upholstery, Mr Armstrong.'

'It won't melt.'

He was mocking her own earlier comment, but she didn't mind. His voice was deep and soothing —how could she ever have thought him dangerous?

He started to nose the car on down the road, through the curtains of rain. 'Call me Mike.'

Mike Armstrong. While lightning flashed and thunder rumbled further off, Helen wondered why the name was so familiar. In spite of the relief of finding her mother here, she was still disorientated. It had all happened so quickly. A menacing figure, a demon, had become rescuer and friend between one thunderbolt and the next. She needed time to catch up.

Meg turned in her front seat. 'Mike and Will are business acquaintances.'

'And friends,' Mike Armstrong added, 'I hope.'

Helen wondered what business he might have with a simple hill farmer like Will Purvis. In those clothes, with this car, he seemed far too rich to be an agricultural salesman.

She realised that her senses were full of the man. His bulk. His dark hair, which had looked like horns and now showed merely as storm-tousled. His tweed jacket with its clean, mossy scent. His big, capable hands on the steering-wheel.

She shivered, remembering how one of those hands had gripped her arm. Under the waxed cotton and the wool of her sleeves, she could almost feel an afterglow from the contact.

Which was absurd. She straightened in her seat. 'Do I gather—er—Mike——' she hesitated over the name '—you're a visitor to the area?'

'Not exactly. I've been seeing your mother all year, at Milburn and Harkness.' He named the solicitors' where Meg worked as secretary. 'Talking to her about your life up here has set me thinking——'

'We'll leave that till we get back,' Meg put in hastily.

'Leave what?' Helen leant forward, struck by a new and horrible suspicion. 'What's going on?'

She stared in alarm at this Mike Armstrong, with his rich clothes and his rich car and his easy, polished manner. Wasn't he enough to sweep any woman off her feet? Even her level-headed mother, who after all had been a lonely widow for ten years?

From her corner, she took in once more the high-cheekboned, strong quarter-profile etched against the streaming glass. He couldn't be more than twenty-seven or eight—only six or seven years older than herself. But there sat Meg beside him, dark-haired, slim and vital in spite of her forty years. These days, lots of men found older women attractive...

'You're not planning to marry?' she blurted out, unable to bear the thought a minute longer.

Mike Armstrong brought the car to a halt, and turned to stare at her.

'Really, Helen!' Meg's laughter, breaking the astonished silence, had a reassuringly genuine ring.

'I'm extremely flattered,' Mike said with a quizzical smile, 'but it's a little early——'

'And a lot too late,' Meg broke in gently.

Helen knew what that meant. Neither of them would ever forget her father, and the cruelly short years they'd had before that motorway pile-up. Even now, ten years later, she felt her parents' love for each other and for her, a shining warmth which stayed with her wherever she went. How could she have so blundered, reminded her mother so needlessly of all they had lost?

'I'm sorry,' she murmured.

Meg offered a hand across the back of her seat. Helen took the hand and squeezed it, and Mike Armstrong, the tension broken, resumed their journey.

'I don't often get a free Saturday,' he threw comfortably over his shoulder, 'so I was glad of the chance to have a look round.'

'I wish the rain had held off for you,' Helen exclaimed.

'I take what weather I'm given.'

Intrigued at the possibility of a kindred spirit, she stared at the back of his head. His hair was drying now, and bouncing into new little tufts at the nape of his neck. She glanced in the driving-mirror and found his eyes, those deep-set eyes, returning her gaze with equal interest.

'So that's how you came to be calling on Will?' she asked.

'More or less. We had things to settle, too.'

Once more she wondered what they could be, and smiled at her own inquisitiveness. 'It was good of you to leave them and bring us home.'

'No problem.' He inclined his head courteously, eyes on the road. 'I told you, I wanted to look round anyway.'

'However little you mind the weather,' she objected, 'you'd hardly choose to be sightseeing in this downpour, would you?'

'I'm not here for the sightseeing.'

'Northumberland's a very beautiful county.' She sprang at once to the defence of her beloved homeland. 'Lots of people do come here on holiday.'

'Mm.' He wouldn't be distracted from the wet road, but the sound showed agreement. 'The Cross Keys, where I'm staying in Linford, is full to the rafters.'

'They come for the fishing, this time of year. I hope the weather soon clears for them.' Helen sat up, professional instincts alerted by the mention of the hotel. 'Are you comfortable at the Cross Keys?'

'That's enough of the hostess act,' Meg broke in with a smile. 'He isn't one of your customers, bossy-boots.'

Helen gave her mother a long-suffering look. If only she wouldn't use that childish nickname in front of strangers. 'I work right next to the Cross Keys,' she explained to Mike Armstrong. 'In the Tourist Information Bureau.'

'Where she spends all her time telling people what a perfect county this is,' Meg added.

'Well, it is.' Helen allowed no argument on that. 'Don't you think so...Mike?' She felt strange, calling him by his first name when only minutes ago... She crushed down the thought.

'I certainly do.' Changing gear at the top of the hill, he glanced briefly round at the heather-clad slopes, the wide sky, the ragged drifts of rain-cloud, then met her eyes again in the mirror. 'But then, I like wild places.'

'We've a lot more than just the moors.'

'I know.'

'Have you been to Lindisfarne?'

'Not yet. I will, though.' He didn't look round, but his voice was light, as if he might be smiling. 'I like the idea of a place that only joins up with the land when the tide's out.'

'Wait till you see it. It's fantastic!'

'So it deserves its name of Holy Island?'

'I'll say. And then there's Cragside, and the Roman wall, and the Kielder Dam——'

'Whoa there!' He was laughing openly now, in much the same way her mother had done a moment earlier. 'All in good time. The nice thing is, they're all an easy car-journey from here.'

'That's just what I'm always saying,' she agreed, forgiving the laughter because of the way he was sharing her enthusiasm. 'This is a marvellous place to live.'

'Storms and all.' Meg brought her daughter back to earth.

Mike Armstrong geared down for the final hill. 'The storms are all part of it.'

'You...' Helen felt strangely hesitant. 'You really like them, then? You weren't just saying that?'

Slowing for the granite gateposts of Thornton Pele, he laughed once more. That laugh told Helen, clearly and finally, that he would never 'just say' anything.

'Did you think I was only being polite?'

'N-not exactly,' she murmured, confused. 'I mean, yes, of course you *were* polite....' Realising she was only making things worse, she sought for a distraction. 'If you like storms, perhaps you should come up to our third floor, for a proper view of this one.'

'Why not?' Meg agreed as they turned into the short drive. 'In fact, I expect Mike would enjoy seeing over the house, Helen.'

As they edged between the tossing rhododendrons, Helen wondered at herself. She didn't usually invite casual visitors to their top floor to enjoy the view. But then, they had so few visitors of any kind, let alone mystery business friends of Will Purvis.

'And you can just stop being so nosy about that,' she told herself with an inward grin. She knew very well that the Will Purvis transaction, or a version of it, would very soon be out for all to hear on the Linrother grapevine.

'You know,' Mike Armstrong had brought the car to a halt before the gold-brown, many-windowed house, 'I feel I knew this place before I ever heard of it.'

'Perhaps you've read of it?' Meg suggested.

'It would have to be an old book, then,' Helen informed them both. 'Nobody writes about it these days.'

'I'm not one for old books much.' Mike Armstrong went on staring at the imposing, two-hundred-year-old façade. 'I like old houses, though. Especially this one.'

'You do?' Helen saw why her mother had taken to him. 'I hope you'll like the inside as much.'

'I'm sure I will.'

Meg opened her door. 'I'll get in, and make the tea.' She scrambled out of the car and through the rain. Between the worn, fluted pillars of the portico, the studded front door opened to her key, and she disappeared beyond it.

Helen sat tight. 'You really feel you know Thornton Pele?'

He turned to face her. Once more she was aware of that saturnine half-profile, the etched lines of nose and cheek and eyebrows. 'It's as if I dreamed it.'

'Oh!' she breathed, enchanted. 'It *is* a place to dream of.'

'Or as if I belonged here.'

She cooled at once. 'It's belonged to the Thorntons ever since it was built.'

His head jerked round. After a measuring glance, he gave her a small, ironic nod. 'I stand corrected.'

'Oh, but I didn't mean——'

'Won't your mother be waiting for us?'

He gestured at the front door, left unlatched by Meg. With an uncomfortable feeling of having been somehow worsted, and now having to do his bidding, Helen slid out of her seat and dashed for the portico.

Watching him close the car and make his own run for cover, she drew a quick breath. She already knew he was tall—she wouldn't easily forget that heart-stopping figure looming over her in the thunderstorm. But until this moment she hadn't been able to observe his springy, athletic stride, the grace of a big man who could move lightly even as he pulled the tweed jacket tight over his chestnut-brown sweater.

She turned away to push at the door. 'Here we are, then.'

And dismal enough the great hall looked, in the watery grey light. Helen had swept the bare parquet that morning, and had let in air through the one mullioned window which could be opened, but still it seemed dank and desolate.

Mike Armstrong was looking round intently, and not with distaste. On the contrary, his face showed an eager interest. 'It's in amazingly good shape.' He indicated the complex coat of arms above the fireplace, the panelled walls, the series of tall windows. 'You must spend half your life on step-ladders, looking after it.'

'It's good exercise,' she said quickly, and relaxed as she realised that he wasn't criticising. Indeed, he was admiring their efforts on the place. Sighing, she threw her head back to stare at the moulded ceiling. 'Great-Grandfather Thomas hung art nouveau chandeliers there. Imagine how funny they must have looked.'

'I don't believe they would.'

She blinked. Nobody contradicted her over Thornton Pele. Then she saw that he was staring beyond her with undisguised admiration. Turning to see what had impressed him so, she realised it was the great staircase, wide and shallow to the half-landing, then dividing in opposing flights to the next floor.

'Those marvellous curves,' he breathed, eyes moving from one oak banister to the other. 'They'd take anything.'

'I can't see them taking those fussy chandeliers.' But she liked his praise. 'Not mixed with the antique swords and guns, and regimental badges, and Indian brassware.'

'Maybe those were what was wrong.'

'They were family!' She regretted her indignant tone at once. She didn't often have a chance to share her delight in this beloved home. 'There were pictures, too,' she added timidly, hoping she hadn't annoyed him again. 'Though nothing really valuable.'

She let out another light, unconscious sigh. If the pictures had been valuable, maybe she and her mother, the last of the Thorntons, would have had a little more to spend on the house.

'Landscapes?' The question was gentle, as if he understood.

'Some,' she responded eagerly. 'The sea, the moors, the castles. And up there——' she flung an arm at the half-landing '—we used to have a Sargent portrait of my great-grandmother.'

'It's a great place for a beautiful woman.'

Only, he was no longer looking at the staircase. And she couldn't meet those deep-set eyes, she wasn't ready. She'd never been ready for any man, much less for this...this invasion, this presence, this devil on the hunt for her inner self.

She turned abruptly, and set off across the echoing floor. 'This way.'

The door beneath the staircase fitted perfectly into the panelling, and was invisible until she opened it. She pulled it outwards, revealing moth-eaten green baize on its other side and a narrow flight of stone stairs leading down from it.

'Could you just wait here a minute?' she asked, and pattered down in search of her mother.

Meg had switched on the light in the long corridor, and was arranging her damp raincoat on its hanger. 'Don't forget to put your wet things over the Aga.'

'Couldn't we have tea in the morning-room?' Helen suggested in a lowered voice. 'It's not too bad up there——'

'Certainly not,' Meg interrupted with decision. 'And I wish you'd stop calling it the morning-room, as if we had twenty others to choose from.'

'Even if we haven't, I'd like to do the place justice.'

'We'll manage that down here, and not freeze our noses off.'

'It's only October,' Helen retorted quickly, to quell her inner vision of Mike Armstrong's narrow, aquiline nose. 'And I'd light the fire.'

'One fire won't do much, after two years without.' Meg closed her mouth to show that the argument was over, then let it relax in a smile. 'Cheer up. We're tidy enough here.'

'I suppose so.' Helen returned with dragging feet to the stone stairs. 'You'd better come down, Mike. This——' she bit on the word like a bullet '—is where we live now.'

Leading him into the low-arched span of the old servants' hall, she glanced round. At least her mother had lit the rose-shaded lamp, so their sitting-corner, with its television and Meg's knitting on the old dresser, looked warm and welcoming.

'Over here.' She led the way to it and offered him one of the two rose-cushioned rocking-chairs.

'Thanks.' His gesture seemed to say he was too interested to sit down, and he remained standing on the worn Wilton rug. 'I thought so. You're built into the side of the hill, so you're not shut up in the dark down here.'

Helen looked out of the two windows. One showed the gold-brown stone walls of the kitchen garden, the raspberry canes a tangled ruin and the gnarled apple trees tossing in the wind. From the other, the moor dropped away steeply to the woods of the Lin valley, cloudy now with the edges of the storm.

'I wish you could see it in decent weather.'

'I like it now.'

'You really do?' She glanced at him curiously, interested once more in this love of wildness which they shared.

'Whoever built this place,' he commented, 'must have been a thoughtful employer.'

'Adam Thornton,' she agreed, pleased. 'He was known for it.'

'So he gave all the below-stairs rooms this outlook?'

'The butler's pantry, anyway, and the sewing-room.'

'She means our bedrooms,' Meg called from the sink where she was filling the kettle. 'Though she only stays in the sewing-room for the summer. Then she moves into the boot cupboard.'

Helen cursed her transparent skin which let the pink blaze in her cheeks so easily. Bad enough that a stranger should see the way they had to live here, without giving him the sordid details. 'It's very big, for a boot cupboard,' she explained. 'And it gets the warmth from the range.'

'Speaking of which,' Meg untied the pulley which lowered the old-fashioned drying-frame, 'give me that coat, and then you can go and change.'

'I'm nearly dry, under my top things.' Helen was suddenly aware of a warmth, almost a glow, at her back. It was Mike Armstrong, helping her out of her Barbour. She started a little at her mother's voice, which came to her as if from a great distance.

'Nearly dry, indeed.' Meg took charge of the Barbour. 'Your trousers are sopping.'

'Only at the knees, where the rain caught them.'

'Go and change, at once.'

'But ...' Helen let her objection trail off, wondering why she was so reluctant. Could it be the warmth of the kitchen which drew her? Or could it be that other warmth, the glow that she instinctively felt was so dangerous?

'To the boot cupboard.' Meg pointed.

Helen moved to the door, but paused there to respond with dignity, 'To my winter bedroom.'

It really wasn't a bad little room, even if it did look out on nothing but a high wall. It took her bed with space to spare, and if hints of ancient turpentine and linseed oil lingered in its store-cupboard, well, they kept away the moths.

She selected a dry pair of jeans from the racks which had once held Thornton footwear, and changed quickly. Then she turned to the tall pier-glass she had moved in here with her.

She couldn't see much of her reflection. Most of the yellowing glass was covered by the beloved midnight-blue party dress on its hanger, hooked to the top of the mirror's mahogany frame for want of a better place. She hadn't worn the dress yet, but the enjoyable sight of it, full of potential, helped her drift off to sleep each night.

Derek had always liked her in dark blue. That was why she'd saved up for this treasure, because she'd hoped she could wear it with Derek. Against all sense, she'd hoped he might come back and take her out to dinner.

'How strange.' She lifted a fold of the soft wool skirt. 'I've never admitted that to myself before.'

Because it was impossible, especially now that he was settled so happily in London. They'd agreed two months ago, on her twenty-first birthday, that their year-long, on-off engagement had been a mistake. She'd known it, only it had left her life so empty, she'd never been able to accept it before.

And now, she could.

'I haven't thought of him for hours,' she realised with surprise. 'I wonder why?'

And because she knew the answer to that, her mind rushed her away from it. Embarrassed, she let go of the dress and took refuge in small, ordinary actions.

Perhaps this old green sweater was rather damp after all. She dropped it with the discarded jeans, and decided that it wouldn't hurt to air her best full-sleeved blue top, which exactly matched her eyes. And normally she would have plaited her still-wet hair, but plaits were so severe. Just this once, she would leave her hair loose round her shoulders. Its coolness bobbed against her neck as she made her way back to the kitchen.

'Over here, love,' Meg called from the great scrubbed table. 'I was telling Mike how we managed to keep this, and the dresser.'

'They wouldn't have fetched much.' Helen hung her damp sweater and soaked jeans on the rack. 'Though they've been here for generations. All the servants used to eat at that table.'

'And I hope they knew how lucky they were,' Meg said comfortably. 'Not having to freeze in those draughty rooms above stairs. Come and have a drop scone.'

'She's a marvel, your mother.' Mike took another as he spoke. 'She made them in minutes.'

'I did have the batter ready.'

'Having things ready is one of the reasons you're a marvel,' Helen told her mother affectionately.

She was surprised how good the table looked. No cloth they owned was big enough to cover it, but Meg had spread the best blue linen cornerways, and had set out the willow-pattern china and the pewter teapot, its dents hidden by an embroidered cosy.

'So Helen's father and I turned this into a family room,' Meg went on, as if taking up where she had left off. 'She often played round and under this table when she was small.'

Helen accepted the proffered cup and saucer, and spoke quickly to head off possible stories about her childhood. 'You look as if you're ready for more tea—er—Mike?'

'Yes, please.' He held out his cup. 'And I'll try that heather honey now, if I may.'

Helen passed the stoneware pot on its willow-pattern saucer. 'It's from our own bees.' She nodded through the window at the bee-skeps sheltered by the wall of the kitchen garden.

'Delicious.' He helped himself liberally. 'It smells of summer on the moor. Which reminds me, what about this scented ghost you've got here?'

Helen exchanged a smile with her mother. 'So you haven't debunked it yet?'

'I was just going to,' Meg told her. 'But you can have first go, if you like.'

'Right,' Helen began with relish. 'In 1825, we had a kitchenmaid called Bridget. A clever girl, who learnt everything the cook could teach her——'

'Or so we suppose,' Meg interrupted. 'Sorry, love.'

'Specially on herbs and spices,' Helen continued. 'She was so good with those, some thought she was a witch.'

'I didn't say make it up,' Meg warned.

Helen stared reproachfully at her mother, but nevertheless cut her narrative short. 'Well, in 1827, Bridget disappeared overnight. No trace of her, except just——'

'Except she sent word weeks later,' Meg put in. 'From Morpeth, where she'd married her childhood sweetheart.'

'And for that she had to run away in the night?' Mike Armstrong asked in humorous bewilderment.

'She'd had a baby,' Helen explained.

'So she took off and sorted things out? Good for her.'

'She was that kind of lady,' Meg said. 'She went on to have a big family, and run a pie shop.'

'Mother!' Helen burst out wrathfully. 'Bridget isn't much of a ghost, but you don't have to turn her into a family pie shop.'

Smiling, Meg lifted a lock of Helen's damp red hair and let it fall. 'Helen would love a real Gothic ghost.'

'We have Bridget's scent,' Helen pointed out, 'and it isn't of veal and ham pies.'

'No, it's...' Mike Armstrong paused. 'It's nutmeg, isn't it?'

'Always here, for the right people.' Helen shot another reproachful look at her mother. 'Bridget must have made an infusion of it. There's an old idea that it helps in childbirth.'

'The whole kitchen smelt of it, the morning after she left.' Meg hesitated, as if owning to a weakness.

'You know these stories. But, well, there *is* still a breath of it, now and then.'

'It isn't just now and then,' Helen argued, as she had many times before. 'It has a definite pattern to it...' She paused. She knew she was right—everything pointed to it. Her parents had known the Thornton Pele scent of nutmeg so well during their marriage, they had taken it for granted. Yet she, who so much wanted to, never had.

'I haven't smelt it once,' she told her mother wistfully. 'Not even with Derek.'

'You and your theories. It could be mice, rot, anything.' Meg stood up, glanced out of the window at the wind-torn clouds, and carried the teapot to the sink. 'If you want to take Mike over the house, you'd better start now before it's dark.'

CHAPTER TWO

'HEAVENS, what a view!'

Mike Armstrong strode to the dormer window. His broad back cut off some of the light, but through the other, west-facing window a thin beam of late sun played across the many-cornered attic-room.

'You can see for miles,' he observed. 'Well beyond Will's place.'

'Pele Farm.' Helen stared wistfully past him to the familiar spread of fields and moor under the restless sky. 'Until sixty years ago, it used to be ours.'

'At least you must be glad to see it in such good hands.' He turned, and glanced round from one posy-patterned wall to another. 'When did you say this room was last used?'

'About forty years ago, I suppose.'

'You'd never guess it'd been that long.'

'We try to check it over, open windows, keep things clean—— '

She broke off with a start of surprise. He had leapt into the air and come down hard, with all his weight. He moved to the middle of the room, and jumped again.

'Not a millimetre's give, anywhere.' He stared at the floor in wonder. 'These boards must be extraordinarily well-braced.'

'This is an extraordinarily well-built house.'

She bit back her annoyance. Who did he think he was, coming here and jumping on their floor-boards? And he must be quite fourteen stone. It would serve him right if he hit his head on a slope of the ceiling.

However, no such luck. He managed that great height with uncanny ease, she noted with unwilling admiration. By now, far too interested in what he was doing to be aware of her irritation, he had dropped smoothly to give the floor a ringing knock.

'There's no worm or rot, if that's what you're looking for,' she informed him, frostier than ever. 'Adam Thornton would only use the best-weathered timber.'

'The best of the best,' he agreed admiringly as he rose and dusted his hands. 'Oh. Sorry.' His dis-arming smile was exactly as it had been ten minutes ago, after he'd tapped the bathroom skirting with his key. 'I get carried away. The condition of this place is amazing.'

'We have kept it in good shape,' she couldn't help responding to his enthusiasm. 'Though it hasn't been easy——'

She bit off the rest of the sentence. She wasn't going to speak of the sacrifices, not to a stranger. Those holiday hours spent cleaning and painting and polishing, the invitations refused because yet another job on the house needed doing or super-vising, the endless maintenance bills which had all been met somehow—those things were strictly family. Better to change the subject.

'The nanny used to sleep here, with the youngest child always in there.' She gestured towards the connecting archway.

'Do I see Winnie-the-Pooh wallpaper?' He walked through the archway and stood looking about him.

She joined him, smiling at his obvious pleasure. 'They put it on before my father was born.'

'We had something like it for PS, when she was younger. Our baby,' he added in fond explanation. 'Real name, Patricia Sarah, but nobody ever calls her that.'

Helen felt suddenly small, chilled, miserable. Why had it never occurred to her that this man, with his looks, his money, his habit of command, would already have a woman in his life? Not only a woman, but a child—he must be married.

'H-how old is P-Patricia Sarah now?' She had to know.

'Hm?' He had crossed to the cast-iron fireplace, and looked up abstractedly from its blue-patterned tiles. 'She's...' he paused, working it out '...coming up fifteen.'

Fifteen! He must be older than he looked.

'That's right.' He nodded, satisfied with his calculations. 'Twelve years younger than me. My parents' afterthought—that's why we call her PS.'

'She's your sister?'

'What did you think she was?' His head snapped up.

'You called her your baby.'

'I see.' He straightened to face her, eyes candid yet seeing deeper than would bear thinking about. 'No, I'm not married. Or engaged to be married. Or even——'

'You don't have to tell me,' she cut in hastily.

'I think I do.'

Fixed with that level gaze, she had to drop her own. 'You seem very interested in our fireplace.'

'I am.' He stooped to its cast-iron wreaths and garlands, the blue and creamy white glazed ceramic. 'It would be an ornament anywhere. Have you ever thought of living up here?'

'You can't cook on that.' She surveyed the pretty fireplace in depression. 'At the moment, you can't even light it. The chimney has a crack.'

'Soon mended.'

'And what about hauling logs or coal up three floors?'

'What kind of talk is that, from a descendant of —which Thornton did you say built this place?'

'Adam,' she snapped, nettled at his casual forgetfulness.

'Adam Thornton. The man who thought of everything.' He slid aside the hatch door next to the chimney-breast. 'I take it nursery meals came up in this service lift?'

'Not meals—there's one in the schoolroom for those.' She took hold of the stout pulley. 'This was for linen, aired clothes, that kind of thing. Would you like us to pull it up?'

'Allow me...' He sprang to help her.

She snatched her hand from under his, but already the heat of the brief contact had shot through her. Cheeks flaming, she covered the hand with her other as if to cool it.

'Here it comes.' All unaware of her agitation, he settled the two-shelved wooden lift at its opening. 'Hardly even a creak, after all these years.'

'It's s-seasoned oak.'

'A masterpiece of engineering.' He turned to her in triumph. 'And you're wondering how to bring... Are you all right?'

'C-certainly I am.'

'You're shivering. You did get pretty wet.'

'I'm not c-cold.'

She wasn't. The wind had fallen, and though a few drifts of rain still pattered on the window, the air was mild. And with her blood racing, surging, pounding like this in her heart and throat, she didn't think she'd ever be cold again.

Nevertheless, he stripped off his jacket. 'Here.' He wrapped her in it. 'Does that help?'

'I told you,' she began, 'I'm not ...'

She couldn't go on. That fresh, mossy scent was all round her, rising on the warmth his body had left in the tweed until her brain swam with it. For the life of her she could do nothing but nestle into it and pull it close, revelling in its softness. Only when she found her cheek stroking the collar did she come to herself, and hastily raise her head.

'Oh, well.'

She knew how graceless she sounded. Worse, how drowsy and off guard, but it was the best she could manage. She couldn't look at him, only let him draw nearer, nearer.

'I've been wanting to do that,' he told her softly, 'ever since I first set eyes on you.'

She fixed her mind on the loops and twists of yarn in that huge chestnut sweater. Suddenly, it seemed to be mopping up all the light in the room.

'Do what? Lend me your coat?'

'Wrap you up, and put you somewhere warm to dry.'

Pride forced her at last to meet those deep-set eyes. 'I was fine really, you know. Well on my way home.'

'Marching along like a...a little half-drowned ginger cat.'

The spell broken, she glared at him. 'Charming!'

'Very,' he murmured.

And she was caught all over again. Why had she never noticed that cleft chin before? Or how dark his eyes were, almost black under those black eyebrows, that black, springy hair? Or how his mouth, his long, sensuous mouth, had a curve at one corner which told, plain as words, of a deep understanding of the arts of pleasure?

'Very charming indeed,' he repeated.

Slow, careful, patient as a man winning the trust of a wild creature, he raised a hand. She turned to watch it in alarm, but he only cupped it an inch from her head, as though warming himself on her bright hair. She stood paralysed, washed about by that fresh, mossy scent, knowing with humiliating certainty that she could be his for a movement or a touch.

Which never came. It was she who pulled away, and it almost hurt, as if some living cord had begun to form between them. He dropped his arm, unsmiling, and watched her slip from his jacket.

'I really don't need this, thank you.' She handed it over.

He accepted and shrugged into it. 'You know best.'

He didn't sound as if he thought she knew best about anything. She wanted to answer back, to challenge the unspoken criticism, but couldn't. Instead, she made for the door with a little manu-factured cough. 'Shall we move on?'

Leading the way into the white-painted corridor, she opened door after door. From this side, they could see down to the holly-hedged front garden and the low, ruined walls of the old pele tower.

'Fancy having one of those in your garden,' he exclaimed. 'Was that built by the Thorntons, too?'

She nodded, smiling. 'In the fifteenth century. We were farmers then, with herds to keep safe from the Scots.'

The small room on the other side of the corridor looked on the kitchen garden, the Lin valley, and the moors beyond.

'So much space.' He stood straight and breathed deep. 'Up here, you're free as a bird.'

'I wish it were that simple,' she began sharply, and checked herself as she took in his expression of unguarded longing. 'You really like it that much?'

'I like it very much indeed. Does that seem so strange?'

'Well, n-no.' To her annoyance, she found she was blushing again under that steady, open scrutiny. 'I m-mean, I like it very much myself, b-but then, I belong here.'

'I could belong here too.'

She turned from him quickly. 'Come and see Bridget's room.' She opened the last door. 'This is where she slept. She shared it with one of the housemaids...'

She fell silent, realising she had been gabbling like a second-rate guide. Yielding to her old childhood curiosity, and because it gave her an excuse to move further away from him, she walked to the far wall and sniffed. But it always had been hopeless, and it still was. No nutmeg.

'No nutmeg.' His voice from the doorway echoed her thoughts. 'So you still don't qualify?'

She jerked to face him. 'What do you mean?'

'This theory of yours.' He leaned comfortably against the door-jamb. 'Would it be something to do with being in love?'

'Has my mother been making fun of it again?'

'She never mentioned it.'

'Then how——?'

'You told me yourself. No, not on purpose,' he went on as she tried to protest. 'It was in your voice, when you spoke of a guy called Derek.'

She stiffened. Derek was in her past, a hopeless episode. But her memories of him were hers alone, private to herself. How dared he read more into her words than she had actually said?

'I know, I know.' He put a hand up like a peace signal. 'It's none of my business. All I'm asking about is the theory.'

'Oh.' She gathered her wits. 'Well. Yes, that is the general idea.'

'So anybody who's in love gets to smell Bridget's nutmeg?'

'N-no,' she began reluctantly. 'Not exactly.'

She'd been in love with Derek. Hadn't she? She'd been sure, until he'd started making those plans to go away for the weekend. Why had she then drawn back, offered excuse after excuse?

'It has to be *real* love.' She spoke too quickly, to shut out this question she had never been able to answer. 'The kind that lasts. The kind my parents had for each other...'

She trailed off. Here she was again, discussing Thorntons with a stranger. No, Mike Armstrong didn't seem like one, but that was because he wasn't behaving like one. Look at him now, standing still, breathing deep, so infuriatingly satisfied she might have just given him a present.

'So Bridget's nutmeg means a love that's going to last?'

'I s-suppose so.'

'And you can't smell it?'

She whirled away to the window, refusing to answer. The question seemed to sum up, in so many words, how shallow and unfulfilled she always felt herself to be.

'Ah, well.' He stayed by the doorway, tolerantly amused. 'You're still very young.'

'I most certainly am not!' she retorted, more irritated than ever. 'Why, I've been out with——' she made a mental count '—at least four men, just since Derek.'

She turned to face him, one hand behind her back so that he couldn't see her crossed fingers. It wasn't four men but three, and two of those, visitors met through her job, much too clearly on the make. The third had been shy, middle-aged Will Purvis, who had taken her and Meg to Alnwick Castle Tournament.

Luckily, he didn't seem about to pursue the subject. He was glancing out at the darkening sky.

'You need to go on somewhere?' she asked, sensitive to any idea that she might be wasting his time.

He shook his head. 'Not particularly. Not until...' He paused, giving her a thoughtful stare. Once more she was drawn to those fathomless eyes, which lingered on her face as if searching for something.

She reminded herself of her role as hostess. 'Then perhaps you'll have a sherry?'

'Thanks, I never drink when I'm driving.' He stood aside from the doorway with a small, commanding motion of his head. 'I'd appreciate a chat with you, though.'

Before she knew it she was obeying, letting him shepherd her to the stairs. Descending, she remembered those hints her mother had dropped hours ago of something this man had to tell her. What with the storm, and that lightning-flash, and then her own outrageous guessing, she'd been so flustered that she'd forgotten it until now.

'I take it my mother already knows what this is about?' she asked as they drew level on the last grand flight.

He nodded, his words echoing through the still air of the great hall. 'She says it's entirely your decision.'

'Decision?' She craned round, but his features had blurred in the rapidly advancing dusk. 'What decision?'

'We'll talk about it in a minute.'

'Just as you like,' she exclaimed in irritation as they crossed the wide, shadowy space.

'No, it has to be as *you* like.' He opened the concealed basement door with serene politeness, and stood back for her. 'But we need to discuss it formally.'

She reached into the dark stair-well and switched on the light. The yellow glow showed him all cool confidence. This, she realised with a new surge of dissatisfaction, was the natural way for him to be. Shrugging, she went ahead of him down the stairs.

Meg had been waiting for them. She stopped beating eggs at the worktop, put down the hand-whisk, and came to the table. 'Sit down, both of you.' She pulled the overhead light down to eye-level, and settled opposite them in the rosy shadows. 'Time to put it to her, Mike.'

'What is this, for heaven's sake?' Helen asked with a sense of foreboding. 'What have you been cooking up together?'

He rested both hands in the table's bright ring of light. 'It isn't like that.'

Helen stared at the well-kept hands with growing resentment. He was as much at home here as if he had brought his own element with him. She could almost see, in the warm dimness round him, a rich boardroom full of urbane colleagues and attentive secretaries. The rough-grained wood under his hands might have been shining mahogany, set out with blotters and carafes and glasses.

'What I have in mind,' he began, 'is that I might make you an offer for Thornton Pele.'

'What?' Helen turned to her mother in horror. 'You've let him think he could buy this place?'

'I'd rather you didn't speak of me as if I weren't here,' he told her with a hint of chill in his voice.

'At least hear him out, Helen,' Meg pleaded.

He glanced from one to the other, and, when he was sure that Helen had stilled, he continued. 'Naturally, you'd want to go on living here. We'd organise that.'

'Very good of you.'

'The top floor's perfect for it.' His manner was firm, as if experienced in keeping discussions on the right lines. 'I'd turn it into two flats. You'd have one——'

'And you'd have the other,' she finished for him.

'That's the general idea.'

'And belong here. So this is what you meant.'

'The rest would become a hotel,' Meg explained. 'Aren't you a little bit interested, to think of it all being lived in again?'

'A *hotel*!' Helen stared at her mother in disbelief. 'You call that having the house *lived* in?'

Meg looked at Mike Armstrong, and shrugged.

'Try considering it.' He frowned, a little rebuking. 'It would be a very special kind of hotel.'

'It practically was one, at the turn of the century,' Meg reminded Helen.

'It was not!' She glared back. 'Great-Grandfather's house parties weren't commercial——'

'Maybe they should have been,' Meg said grimly, 'seeing what they did to the family finances.'

'So you've been talking about those, too?' Helen stared accusingly at her mother, who shrugged.

'Everybody knows how we live here. Tell her,' Meg went on to Mike Armstrong, 'what you're prepared to offer.'

He did, and she couldn't suppress her gasp at the sum.

'Subject to survey,' he added.

'Survey.' She recovered at once. 'More people jumping on our floorboards?'

He acknowledged the hit with a brief, apologetic grin. 'Rather more scientific than that.'

'No money on earth——'

'When I think,' Meg interrupted, 'how often you've said we need another survey——'

'Not so I could sell.'

'You'd rather hang on to a house that's too big to run, too ordinary for the National Trust, too remote——'

'That's exactly why I like it.' Mike Armstrong's intervention was smooth, practised, soothing, but he had a light in his eyes. 'It's just...' He shrugged, surprisingly lost for words. 'Just perfect. The perfect blend of wildness and peace.'

'Try digging yourself out of the snow every winter,' Meg told him with a sigh, 'and see if you still feel like that about it.'

'Snow! I can't wait to see snow up here.'

'Your guests wouldn't be able to move out of the house.'

'I wouldn't want guests in winter,' he assured her. 'I'd close in the autumn, after the fishermen went home, and stay closed till spring.'

'You're not expecting to make a profit, then?' Helen asked with acid sweetness.

'It isn't profit I'm after, it's a way of living.' He spoke absently, fixed on some private, inner vision. 'You've said yourself what a marvellous place this is to live.'

'That was before I knew——'

'I'd have all the border country around, and a home…' He gave his head a little shake, and found another word. 'A flat, under your roof.'

'So that's why you were so keen on the top floor.' Her anger rose anew. 'You were working this out up there, weren't you?'

He met her eyes with such an open, gentle glance, she had to look away. Staring at her own work-worn hands, tensely interwoven on the table before her, she couldn't shut from her mind what he had just shown her. Through all his cool strength something else had looked out—a need, a longing almost, and a wish to have the longing understood.

'It's no crime,' he almost whispered, 'to dream.'

'It is,' she stiffened her resolution, 'when you dream of taking somebody's home away from them.'

'Come, now.' His voice hardened. 'You told me yourself, nobody's lived in those rooms for forty years.'

'We'd have gas-fired central heating, Helen.' Meg spoke with resignation, her glimpse of paradise fading. 'And Bridget's room would be our kitchen. Imagine, an Armstrong kitchen!'

'Armstrong. That's where I've heard of you.' Helen was at last able to raise her head in an accusing stare. 'You're Armstrong and Son.'

'Guilty. The "and Son", at your service.' He sketched a brief, mocking bow where he sat. 'I gather you don't think much of that, either.'

She shrugged. 'I suppose you're entitled to build your ticky-tacky houses, if you can get people to buy them.'

'Helen!' Meg was scandalised.

'That's a nasty little word,' Mike Armstrong said to Helen. 'My old man built the firm on fair dealing.'

'I should think he did,' Meg agreed. 'Armstrong homes have won prizes all over the country.'

'We've neither of us ever put up anything,' he left a disdainful pause, 'anything *ticky-tacky* in our lives.'

Helen stared helplessly into the dark eyes. She knew she had put herself completely in the wrong, and was already ashamed.

'I rather think,' his tone continued mild, but now had an edge of steel, 'you're going to take it back.'

'All right.' She accepted the penalty almost with relief. 'I'm sorry I used that word. I shouldn't have.'

'That's better,' Meg murmured.

'But neither should you have——' Helen paused, more careful this time '——have come here like a friend, when what you were after was a...a bargain.'

His expression iced over. 'Perhaps you'll leave me to be the judge of what I was after.'

'You've heard what he's prepared to offer, Helen,' Meg put in. 'Do you think you'd get that anywhere else? And we'd still be living here.'

'So would he.'

'A man in the house again.' Meg cast a wistful glance to the photograph on the dresser. 'Would that be so awful?'

'You're forgetting, it wouldn't be just one man.' Helen made a movement as if drawing her non-existent skirts away from Mike Armstrong. 'He'd fill the place with every Tom, Dick and Harry who could afford the price of a room.'

He gave her a wintry smile. 'You picture my project as a sort of flop-house?'

Meg shot him a disturbed glance, then addressed her daughter with rare urgency. 'You're getting carried away again, Helen.'

'What I'm planning,' he went on, clipped and precise, 'is a few guests, each with plenty of room. And they'll be the sort of people who value peace and quiet.'

'You think so?' Helen flung up her head in a new challenge.

'I don't generally make claims I can't back up.'

'So back it.'

'Very well. For a start, they'd pay five-star prices.'

'And that would keep out the rowdies? Some hope, with the kind of people who have money nowadays.'

'Now don't start that,' Meg warned, and turned to Mike Armstrong. 'She means we haven't any.'

'No, I don't,' Helen contradicted. 'Though we should. We'd make better use of it than a lot of the people who have it.'

'Interesting.' His mouth tightened. 'And what exactly would you do with it?'

'I certainly wouldn't try to buy people out of the homes where their families have lived for generations.'

He gave her a freezing, courteous nod. 'But that's still what you *wouldn't* do. Let's have the positive side.'

'Well, I'd . . .' She cast round for ideas. 'I'd . . .'

'Hunt wretched foxes, like John Thornton?' he asked with dangerous smoothness. 'Or bankrupt yourself entertaining the county, like Thomas Thornton?'

'How...how dare you?' Choked with indignation, Helen turned to her mother for support. To her amazed chagrin, she found Meg's lips quirking.

'It's ancient history, darling. Your father often said——'

'What he'd say to family is very different from what he'd say to outsiders!'

'And on that note,' Mike Armstrong pushed back his chair, and rose with an air of finality, 'maybe this outsider had better be on his way.'

Helen stared up at him, alarmed at the mixture of feelings the statement roused in her. She was still furious with him, still wanted to put him down— but she didn't want him to leave.

'It's Helen's house, Mike. I only have the use of it in my lifetime.' Meg, too, had risen with an air of helplessness. 'I warned you how it would be, didn't I?'

'You did.' He accepted her proffered hand with kindness, even with amusement. 'I went ahead entirely at my own risk.'

'If she wants to keep it like this——' Meg glanced round at their makeshift comforts, and sighed '—she has the right.'

Helen rose to join them with an obscure feeling of having lost another round. She'd stayed in her seat, she realised, to try and bring him back to his. But it hadn't worked, and now he was going, while half her angry words bubbled in her unsaid. Well, at least she could throw back his rebuke of a moment ago.

'When you're done talking about me as if I weren't here——' she crossed to the dresser for her torch '—I'll see you out.'

'No need,' he told her, far less indulgent than he had been with her mother. 'I can find my own way.'

'I doubt it.'

'There's no electricity in the great hall,' Meg explained. 'The wiring being what it is.'

'And besides,' Helen threw over her shoulder, 'it's time to bar the door. Against intruders.'

They mounted to the great hall in frigid silence. The torch-beam shone weak and small through the darkness, but Helen used it carefully, holding it down to show where he should walk, and on the door to show where it could be unlocked. It opened to a quiet night where the overgrown bushes rustled the last rain from their leaves in a wind grown soft as spring.

'So the storm's over for the time being.' His tone was neutral. 'And the invader repelled.'

She switched off the torch. 'We Thorntons have always known how to defend our own.'

'Which explains your pele tower mentality.'

'Not a bad thing to have, if the reivers are still about.'

'They're not, but you haven't noticed. Here comes a stranger—are the sheep locked up?' He drove ruthlessly through her protest. 'Here comes a new idea—is the boiling oil ready?'

Maddened, she struggled for words. 'There's a difference between new ideas and vandalism.'

'How would you know? You'd never wait to find out.'

'I've found out all I need to know, thank you.'

'If you mean about my plans, you haven't even asked.'

'I didn't need to——'

'Your mother listened like a reasonable person. But then, she's only a Thornton by marriage, isn't she?'

'Why, you...' She gritted her teeth, furious at her own stammering. This wasn't at all the kind of final interview she'd planned. She stepped back against the half-open door, realised she was retreating, and stiffened her resistance. 'Kindly leave my family out of this.' It wasn't much, but it held up the honour of the Thorntons.

'You see?' His mastery was all the clearer for his easy, derisive tone. 'Family again. You think there was nobody in the Garden of Eden except your own relations.'

'Don't be ridiculous.'

'A pity, because I was getting to like old Adam Thornton.'

'I'm sure he'd be flattered to hear it.'

'But that other Adam——' his voice became a silky murmur '—there's a bit of him in all of us.'

She couldn't mistake his meaning. If the caressing voice hadn't made it clear the strong hand would have, stealing up to her cheek and turning her face to his whether she would or not.

And would she? Of course not! 'Don't you...' she croaked. 'Don't you dare...'

'Dare what?' he demanded in that same dizzying undertone. 'Dare show you why Eve was created?'

She blinked up at the black silhouette against the faintly moonlit garden. The heathery scent of his jacket filled her senses, stronger and stronger, nearer and nearer, until it was all round her, drawing her close and pressing her body to his.

At first, her lips stayed tight shut. Then, hardly knowing how it happened, she tasted his. And then she was delighting in their victory as they took full and welcome possession of her mouth. She felt his hand on her hair, stroking down it to her shoulders, his fingertips delicately exploring her neck, her jaw, her ear. And wherever he touched, a new fire darted through her. She couldn't let it go on, she would be consumed . . .

'Leave me alone.' It came out slurred and reluctant as she dragged herself away.

'Shall I?'

He dropped his arms and took a step back. Released as she had demanded, separated from him as she'd felt she must be, she could hardly bear the loneliness of it.

'Shall I leave you? Is that really what you want me to do, Helen Thornton?'

'What I want you to do,' she fought to recover her sense of independence, 'is mind your own business.'

'A good answer.' He swung away from her. 'I will.'

Chilled, she watched his black, gigantic shadow move to the car and merge with its opening door. He turned for a final glance—up at the house, down to where she stood in the darkness of the porch. As moonlight and blackness slid in odd patterns over the untidy black hair, the great dark eyes, the high-bridged nose, she recalled the flat brilliance of the lightning-flash. And here, just in time, came the crushing last word she'd been seeking.

'When I first saw you,' she called across to him, 'it wasn't Adam I thought of, it was the devil!'

And it didn't crush him at all. He only inclined his head, and asked on a note of amusement, 'Indeed?'

'Out for one of his left-handed bargains.'

'You mean, after more than he's telling?' He sounded reflective, considering the idea more seriously than she had meant it. 'As far as you're concerned, you may be right.'

The car door smoothly closed, the engine murmured into life, and he was gone as finally, as frustratingly as ever Lucifer could have cloaked himself in night.

CHAPTER THREE

'I don't care what you say, he's up to no good.' Helen finished sewing the button on her coat, and snipped the thread.

'All right.' Meg poured out the last of the real, percolated, weekend-breakfast coffee. 'Tell me why Mike Armstrong shouldn't spend the winter in Linrother if he wants to.'

'Because the Armstrongs must be millionaires several times over, that's why.'

'And we don't allow millionaires here?'

Helen banged the lid on the mending basket. 'Moor Cottage is a summer let.'

'It's very pretty.'

'And very small.' Helen drained her coffee without tasting it. 'You wouldn't expect anybody rich to settle there, any more than I would.'

'By small,' Meg stood up to gather things on the tray, 'you mean the kitchen isn't twenty yards wide?'

'It isn't three yards long.' Helen picked up the cereal packets, and set off after her mother to the pantry.

'It's cosy.' Meg glanced at the window-frame as she passed, and sighed. 'We ought to re-putty that, before it rains again.'

'I'll do it. I got the putty yesterday, during my lunch-hour.' Helen opened the pantry's heavy old door, still assembling her arguments. 'Mike Armstrong could live any place he likes.'

'He happens to like Linrother. And Moor Cottage,' Meg set the tray on the marble shelf with an air of resignation, 'happens to be the only house here that's available to him.'

'I'll deal with these.' Helen quickly put the honey and the marmalade in their proper places.

She was relieved when Meg shrugged and departed. In the two weeks since she had turned down the offer for Thornton Pele, her mother had never referred directly to the disappointment. It kept showing, though, in small ways like this.

Whenever it did, Helen was swept with the familiar longing to talk it over with her father. He'd have understood. That was why he'd left her the house direct—because she shared his passionate love of it. After all, Meg was only a Thornton by marriage, as Mike Armstrong had pointed out . . .

Not that *he* counted for anything. Helen slammed the butter on the upper shelf and returned to the kitchen, hoping her mother had found something different to think about.

She had. 'The Wilsons' kitten climbed their roof again,' she said from the earthenware sink. 'Mike had to go up and get it.'

'That kitten's always in trouble. And I wish you wouldn't call him Mike, as if he were a friend.'

'I think of him as one.' Meg ran hot water into a bright orange plastic bowl. 'So do lots of people in the village.'

'He's only been there a week. But then,' Helen worked the pulley to bring the tea-towel within reach, 'anybody can be popular, if they throw enough money around.'

'It isn't a question of money. He's very neighbourly.'

'How?' Helen couldn't resist asking.

'Well, ever since Anne Simon went to hospital for the new baby, he's been taking the twins to school.'

'I'd have done that.'

'He's handier, right next door. And,' Meg sluiced a plate, 'he gave old Mrs Pringle a lift home from Linford, on market day.'

'We could do that any time. Why ever hasn't she asked?'

'Because she'd rather get the bus than hang about waiting for you and me to finish work.'

'Which Mike Armstrong can do whenever he pleases.'

'I hardly think so.' Meg fitted the plate in the wooden rack. 'He works very hard on that site by the river. His staff respect him for it.'

'Do they indeed?' Helen stared suspiciously. 'And how would you know that?'

Meg piled cutlery on the wooden draining-board. 'I called on him yesterday. During my lunch-hour. With,' she scrubbed at a fork, 'with a message from Will.'

'From Will?' Helen forgot the cup she was drying. 'Did it give you any clues? I'm amazed word hasn't got out yet——'

'A *written* message,' Meg said drily. 'But while I was there, Mike took me over the show bungalow. The workmanship's superb.'

Helen stiffened. She knew exactly what her mother was telling her. That same workmanship could be hers, theirs, here in their own home, if she would only sign away her birthright. 'I don't care, it doesn't make any difference...' She stopped, put off by the echo in her own mind.

'You'd never wait to find out' came back to her, in the deep, masculine voice she was trying to forget. Sometimes, especially when she was drifting to sleep, it took over from reality. At those times she not only heard but sensed him—a gentle hand curving near her hair, a clean-scented tweed wrapping round her, and then a warm darkness into which she gladly melted, gladly surrendered her lips...

'For goodness' sake put that cup down,' Meg's voice came as a welcome distraction, 'and get on with this cutlery.'

Helen hastened to pick up the knives and wipe them dry. 'I bought most of the stuff for my cake, yesterday,' she offered as a way of changing the subject.

'The one for the Christmas draw?'

'It's going to be super.'

'You know,' Meg turned to survey her daughter's blue eyes and fine features, 'you're getting more like your father every day.'

'Am I?' Helen darted a quick, pleased smile.

'The same pleasure in small jobs. The same pride——' Meg tensed to the shrill of the telephone. 'That'll be Nora.'

'You answer it, darling. I'll finish here.'

Meg didn't need a second telling. 'Seven weeks to go,' she murmured as she stripped off her rubber gloves and hurried to the dresser to pick up the phone.

Almost as eager, Helen rinsed the dishcloth and hung it to dry without a sound. Meg's younger sister, thirty-eight and radiant with her first pregnancy, always called on Saturdays to assure them that all was well.

And it was. Nora's husband was home for the moment from the oil rig, so her happiness was complete. Delighted, Helen emptied the washing-up bowl with a great whoosh.

By the time the water had sluiced away down the sink, Meg already seemed to be talking of something else. She darted a glance over at her daughter. 'No, he hasn't.'

Helen listened on a wave of irritation. Did they never get tired of discussing Mike Armstrong and his offer? Nora had put her arguments two weeks ago, urging her niece to 'be sensible'.

'Sensible indeed,' Helen fumed as she wiped the bowl.

'. . . can't do that,' Meg was saying. 'I'm the one who has to live here.'

Helen reached for the hand-towel with a pang. Was it really so awful for her mother, living like this?

'Linrother,' Meg went on, 'just isn't that liberated.'

Liberated? What had that to do with anything?

'. . . can't do much about it,' Meg was saying. 'We'll just have to wait and see.'

And you won't see me selling Thornton Pele, however long you wait, Helen silently added.

'. . . maybe Christmas will be the time.'

Christmas? Helen wondered crossly if they thought she'd change her mind once she was full of turkey and plum pudding.

Called to the phone for her turn, however, she melted at the news of the baby's mighty kicks, the equipment slowly gathering in the new nursery, and at Nora's thanks for the fluffy toy she had chosen so carefully. By the time she returned the receiver to her mother, she felt full of energy for her next job.

'I'd better be off.' She glanced at her watch. 'I hope this weather keeps up for the Armistice Day service tomorrow.'

Replacing the phone, Meg glanced out at the perfect autumn sky. 'You're at least going to sell your poppies in sunshine.'

She smiled tenderly at her daughter's retreating back. It was often there, Meg's smile, when she contemplated the straight shoulders, slender neck, and intractable red-gold curls. All were such a perfect expression of the stubbornness within. Helen's more vulnerable side didn't show again until she returned, eyes wide, full mouth soft with uncertainty.

'Is it really so bad for you, living here?' She belted her camel-hair coat over the rounded, womanly lines of her figure. 'I suppose it must be a worry, when you're getting older...'

The rest was lost in Meg's peal of laughter. 'My poor old bones,' she said when she could speak again.

'Oh, I know you're quite young now——'

'On your way, before I start feeling a hundred.'

'You're marvellous—did I ever tell you?' Helen gave her mother a quick hug. 'See you about lunchtime, then.'

She thoroughly enjoyed her rounds with the poppies. Everyone expected her, everyone was ready with money for her collecting-box in return for the stylised Remembrance Day flowers to pin in their lapels.

She went to Pele Farm first, and met Will's new Sheltie pup. Then she drove to the middle of the village, parked outside the church, and carried her tray from door to door. At the Burrells', she helped free a blackbird from the front bedroom, and in every house discussed the size, weight and names of the new Simon baby.

'They must be relieved to have a girl at last,' old Mrs Pringle commented, 'after their three scallywags.'

'Where are they this morning?' Helen asked.

Mrs Pringle nodded at the creamy-brown stone houses on the other side of the road. Sure enough, blood-curdling tribal noises rose from behind the neatly clipped evergreens.

'I'll take over their poppies, then. That'll just about finish my round.' Helen crossed to ring the Simon doorbell.

She hardly heard its two-note tinkle. A tangle of arms and legs erupted from the back garden, and three-year-old Billy pointed a piece of wood roughly shaped like a rifle.

'You be the stage-coach,' ordered one of the twins, a battered miniature stetson hanging by elastic at the back of his neck. 'An' we'll rob you while we're waiting for the Apaches.'

'Sorry, I can't be robbed today. Where's your——?'

A powerful bass roar drowned Helen's question. Mike Armstrong danced into view in a brown, patterned blanket, and clutched his heart theatrically as Billy shot him. 'You got me, Duke.' He began a slow, spectacular collapse.

'You can't die yet.' A twin ran to brace two hands on Mike's chest. 'We have to burn you at the stake.'

'Cowboys,' Helen couldn't resist pointing out, 'don't burn Indians at the stake.'

'We do,' the other twin told her disapprovingly.

'All right, all right.' The Apache straightened up. 'Let me buy my poppy from the pretty lady.'

Helen found that she was blushing and he hadn't even said hello to her yet. Luckily, a toot sounded from the road, sending the boys surging to their father's car. Jim Simon got out, rumpled each fair head in turn, and opened the hatchback.

'Is that our chocolate ices?' a twin asked of the cardboard carton his father was bringing out.

'No, it's Uncle Mike's wine. Stand back a minute.' Jim hefted the carton and tried to step clear of Billy, who was lovingly wrapped round his knees.

'Hang on.' Mike dropped his blanket. 'I'll fetch it.'

'It's all right, I've got it.' Jim tried to move, and Billy yelped, brandishing his rifle club-fashion. 'Stop that, Bill.'

Looking down to speak to his son, Jim tilted the carton. Billy wedged his rifle under it and tilted it further, until bottle clanked against bottle. Mike dashed to the rescue, but before he reached them the carton had lurched sideways and fallen with a crunch of breaking glass. A red stain started to seep through the brown cardboard.

Jim snatched up his son to still his frightened wails. Mike dropped to his knees beside the carton, and Helen set down her tray of poppies and hurried to kneel at its other side, forgetting all their differences in her eagerness to help.

'Keep the boys away, Jim,' she ordered as she drew out a bottle which dripped with wine, but turned out to be undamaged. 'We don't want them cutting themselves.'

'It's not as bad as it sounded.' Mike laid a bottle on its side in the grass. 'Only one broken, as far as I can see yet.'

Jim patted Billy's back, and looked apologetically over the little boy's head. 'I'll replace it.'

'Nonsense. I've still got...' Mike took out the last bottle, and set it triumphantly by the others '...five.'

'Let me help you clear up, then.'

'Don't be silly.' Helen sat back on her heels, the better to assert her authority. 'There's two of us here for that.'

Still kneeling opposite her, Mike Armstrong gave her a quizzical glance, then grinned at his neighbour. 'You heard what the lady said.'

Embarrassed, she shot to her feet. Not that she wanted to get away, she assured herself, but he could deal perfectly well with the wine himself, and hadn't one of the twins said something about ice-creams? Here they were, and other frozen food besides, already glittering with melted frost in the warmth of the car.

'May I help you indoors with this, Jim?' she asked. 'The sooner it gets in your freezer, the better.'

Still, Jim hovered. 'What a way to thank anybody for a morning's babysitting.'

'In you go, cowboys.' Helen shooed the twins ahead of her and her burden. 'Daddy's going to give you your ice-cream now. Come and let me into your house, Jim.'

She carried the supermarket purchases to the Simon kitchen, locked up the car, and handed the keys through the front door to one of the twins.

'Now mind,' she warned sternly, 'they're not for playing with. Take them straight to your father.'

'Do you think he will?' Mike Armstrong called across.

'He'd better.' Helen returned to a front garden grown suddenly, blessedly peaceful. 'What are you doing with my tray?'

'Taking it in my kitchen, so I can buy a poppy.' He stood up with the tray and the collecting-box. 'Tell me, what's the magic for making those three behave?'

Scooping up the soggy carton with its broken glass, Helen considered. 'Ask their mother. She has them at a word.'

'So have you. Leave that—I'll come back for it.'

She shook her head. 'We might as well finish the job.'

'All right. Bring it if you must, but I won't deal with it until after we've had our coffee.'

'Oh.' She hesitated, the carton sticky in her hands. 'I'm not sure——'

'Don't stand there arguing.' He moved round, cutting off her retreat. 'And hold that thing clear, or you'll get wine on your skirt.'

She hastily readjusted her grip on the carton. Thus taken up, she had no answer when he shooed her ahead of him much as she had shooed the twins. They crossed the lawn to Moor Cottage, where she dumped the carton as he told her, outside the kitchen.

'Thank you.' Still holding her tray of poppies, he gestured with his head to the open kitchen door. 'Now come in.'

Resenting his commanding tone, she hesitated again. 'I'm not sure...'

'You want to wash your hands, don't you?'

She looked down at her wine-sticky fingers and shrugged, defeated once more. He set her tray on a worktop, the poppies suddenly small and dark against its flame-pink. A gurgling coffee machine filled the air with promise as he moved past her to the stainless-steel double sink, and turned the tap for her. She held her hands under the water.

'You're ... you're bleeding!' She pointed to the bright trickle from his thumb, yet another red in this riot of reds.

'So I am.' He held it up to examine. 'It must be from the broken glass.'

'It's quite a deep cut.'

'It's nothing.'

'How can you say that?' She turned off the tap, and reached for the towel. 'There are all sorts of infections about.'

'You think so?'

'Specially out of doors.'

'I always——'

He broke off as she took the hand in both of hers. In spite of his casual attitude to the cut he let her inspect it, his skin warm against her own, which was chilled by the cold water.

'Maybe, after all,' he murmured, 'I shouldn't take risks.'

'You certainly shouldn't. Where's your antiseptic?'

'Antiseptic.' He shook his head with a slow, dreamy smile. 'What an old-fashioned girl you are. No, don't do that.'

'Do what?' She had let go his hand to run both taps, mixing for the right temperature. 'We have to wash it.'

'Oh, you can wash it,' he said softly, his voice half-muffled by the rushing, gurgling water. 'I don't mind you washing it.'

He offered the hand back. She took it, and the dreamy smile lengthened, deepened into those enjoying, enjoyable lines she'd hoped to have forgotten.

'As long as you keep holding it.' His other hand stole up to her. 'Keep right on there holding it.'

The noise of running water made everything curiously unreal. It covered all other sounds. When his fingertips stroked the nape of her neck, and her blood leapt to meet them, it didn't seem to matter—you couldn't hear it. You couldn't hear the pulse at the base of her throat either, or the one in the curve of her jaw, each in turn set throbbing by his fingers. Light as snow, hot as flame, covered by that endless, steady rushing, his index finger stole to her mouth and teased its corner.

'Apple blossom,' he whispered, close to her ear. 'A wind from the south. Sunlight through the leaves of a copper beech.'

'A-a-antiseptic?'

She surfaced with an effort, and pulled her head away. He dropped his exploring hand, and once more she felt that cold sense of loss which was beginning to be so horribly familiar. She tried to master it by thinking very hard about germs.

'Antiseptic?' she repeated, firmer and more demanding above the surge of the water, the surge of her blood.

His voice blew warm against her ear. 'Haven't any.'

'Really, Mike!' She violently shook her head. 'What do you expect to do at times like this?'

He wasn't touching her any more. Not touching, yet all round her, cutting her off from everything but that rushing, rushing, rushing, while his voice filled her ear with warmth and softness. 'Kiss it better?'

She grabbed his hand, turned to the sink, and reset the taps. Freezing water spurted over them both in a drenching spray.

He didn't jump back, or swear, or give any sign of being upset. But at least he moved away, crossing the tiny space to the door. Once there he stayed a moment, licking in a drop which had landed on his lip, and meeting her eyes with perfect composure. 'Another time, perhaps?'

'Not in a...'

But he'd gone; she could hear him taking the stairs two at a time. Helen blinked cold water from her eyes, angry as much with herself as with him, and let the icy stream cascade full over the insides of her wrists.

'Hm. Maybe you're right.'

She jumped as she realised he'd returned, the sound masked as ever by the noise of the water. Pulling his sleeves up over tanned, muscular forearms, he claimed the nozzle from her and let the water play over his wrists exactly as she had done.

'You shouldn't hold a guy's hand like that, Helen Thornton. It's like whisky to the Indians.'

'But . . .' she spluttered in helpless indignation. 'It would just serve you right if you got tetanus!'

'Unlikely.' He handed her a deep-brown towel. 'I had an anti-tetanus shot just last week.'

'Oh, you . . .'

She grabbed the towel, glad to hide her face. This, she realised in its luxurious, fluffy depths, must be why he'd gone upstairs, to fetch something to dry them both. He had one for himself, too. Not wanting to dwell on the sight, she looked past him to the five red-stained bottles of Saint-Emilion lined up on the draining-board.

'After I helped rescue your wine for you.'

'You certainly sorted us out,' he agreed with a grin.

'Those who'd let themselves be sorted. At least I can make the Simon boys do as they're told.'

'And that's quite something. Do you think,' he began in a conversational tone, 'they're throwbacks to the Viking raiders?'

She pressed her lips together, unwilling to admit how amused she was by the idea.

'It's not hard to picture them coming ashore to loot the monasteries,' he added, 'while your lot took to the hills.'

'We would not,' she asserted stoutly. 'We'd stand and fight. Though I don't suppose we were here at the time.'

'I thought that was what old families were all about.' He took back her towel, and dumped it with his on the worktop. 'Knowing what their ancestors were up to at any given time.'

'The Thorntons only came south of the border with James the First.' She warmed to her subject. 'Though the farm's mentioned in the Domesday Book.'

He gave a satisfied nod, as if some effect he was after had been achieved. 'Why don't you tell me about it over coffee?'

'I really don't want——'

'The living-room's through there.' He had taken two mugs out of the blazing-pink cupboard, and filled them from the coffee-jug. 'Sugar? Milk?'

'I really don't . . . oh, all right, then. No, and a splash.'

He had a trick of leaving her with nowhere to go but where he intended. She opened the door ahead of him, and in no time at all he had her corralled in a chintz-covered armchair, her coffee on the tiled hearth, a log on the fire, and himself in the matching chair on the other side. At least, she reflected with some satisfaction, at least she still wore her coat, even if it was making her uncomfortably hot.

'I must get some cups and saucers.' He raised his mug. 'This place doesn't provide crockery, so these are all I have at the moment.'

She took up hers, pleased by the lightness and grace of its shell-thin, lustrous brown porcelain.

'A farewell present,' he told her, observing her interest.

'This colour's quite extraordinary.'

'Think so?' He laughed, yet the laugh somehow showed no pleasure. 'To match my eyes, Celia said.'

'Another sister?'

'No.'

She waited for more, but nothing came. Realising how very much she had wanted it, she began talking fast. 'I don't see why men shouldn't have things to match their eyes, same as women . . .'

With an uneasy feeling that she was babbling nonsense, she trailed off and stared at the mug again. It didn't match his eyes anyway, it wasn't deep enough. Or hadn't enough black in it. Or something. She wasn't about to look up and compare.

And perhaps she hadn't been talking nonsense after all. At any rate, he was taking her comment seriously.

'Cele thinks everybody should be above matching anything.'

'She sounds a bit—er—puritanical?' Helen suggested.

'I suppose she is. At any rate, she has high standards, and lives up to them.'

Something in his voice made Helen feel infinitely small and worthless. Who was this Celia, who could make him speak so sadly and with such respect?

'But I didn't bring you in here,' he sipped his coffee, 'to talk about my own . . . affairs.'

Affairs. In that moment, Helen knew beyond any doubt that he had been very much in love with this Celia. Perhaps he still was. Astonished at the misery which seared through her, she drained her coffee too fast, and scalded her tongue. The smart was almost welcome—it brought her to herself. What was that he'd just said?

'Do I gather,' she began, 'that you did bring me in here to talk about something else?'

'Ancestors,' he reminded her lightly.

'And that's all?' Revived by the stinging-hot coffee, she was able at last to look straight at him. 'Nothing else?'

'I think you've probably guessed it.' He set down his mug, and gave her a hard stare. 'I wanted to give you one more chance to change your mind over Thornton Pele.'

'And that's it?' She sat forward in the armchair.

'If I put up the stakes?'

'There isn't that much money.'

'Hm.' He left a long, thoughtful pause. When he spoke again his voice was softer, more tentative. 'Have you ever thought, Helen, that you might find yourself living alone there some day?'

'Of course,' she answered at once. This was something she had indeed thought about, very seriously. 'And my mother will get really old, like Mrs Pringle. But maybe by then——'

'I didn't mean that far in the future.'

She stared at him, puzzled. 'What did you mean, then?'

'You really don't know?' He shrugged, as much at a loss as she had ever seen him. 'We'd better leave it.'

'Leave what?' she demanded in growing indignation.

'Something I should never have started.'

'There's a lot you should never have started.' She glanced pointedly at her watch. 'Thank you very much for the hospitality. Even if it was——' she couldn't resist adding '—to try and get something out of me.'

'Wait. I haven't finished.'

Once more, in spite of her resistance, she found herself doing as she was told. The best she could manage was to stay on the edge of her seat, poised for departure, while he settled back.

'We still haven't talked about ancestors. Did you know mine came from the coast hereabouts?'

'Very interesting.' She glanced at her watch again.

'Fisher-folk, they were, from way back.'

'I can't see——'

'And known for always bringing home their catch.'

'I really can't hang about while you go through your family history.' Helen braced herself to rise.

'If they couldn't land it one way, they landed it another. The Armstrongs are used to getting what they want.'

'I see. Well, they'll never get Thornton Pele.'

'So I gather. But I'm going to have my hotel.'

He was so sure of himself. What did he know, to make him so sure? She hid her sudden uncertainty. 'Not here, you aren't.'

'Here.' He lifted a long roll of papers from the table beside him. 'You can see the plans, if you like.'

'Thanks, that won't be necessary.' She waved them away. 'Where do you think you're going to build it?'

'On the land I'm buying from Will Purvis.'

'Cuddymoor.' She felt sick. 'He's selling you Cuddymoor.'

'Will's glad to get it off his hands,' he confirmed. 'He says it's never been much use to him. I'll plant trees——'

'It's got trees. My hawthorn, my crab-apple.'

'A few scrubby little wind-breaks, and not yours. Not this time.'

'They were when I was little!' Helen couldn't keep the shock, and the passionate appeal, from her voice. 'That low branch of the hawthorn, that was my horse. I used to ride it against the reivers.'

'You did?' He sounded interested, and amused. 'Shall I see if I can keep it for its historic interest?'

'Who are you to make fun of me, you...you wrecker?' She sprang up at last, released by a black wave of fury. 'I'll fight you. I'll rally the village. You'll never build your...your monstrosity.'

'Here we go again.' He rose to join her, sighing. 'How do you know it's going to be a monstrosity?'

'Of course it will be. Why don't you make a...a caravan site, an amusement park, souvenir stalls——'

'Sure, sure,' he interrupted in mock agreement. 'And a factory or two, while I'm about it.'

'You might as well. Seeing that you plan to destroy the village.'

'I'm destroying nothing. I'm improving the site.'

'Oh, yes? Where have I heard that before?'

'If you'll only look at my ideas——'

'Keep those things away from me.' She drew back as if they might contaminate her.

'All right.' He shrugged. 'Will you buy the employment angle? I'll be providing jobs.'

'Jobs for outsiders.'

'Ah, yes. Outsiders. I thought we might get back to that before we'd done.'

'And if you ever finish it, you'll have more outsiders coming to stay in it. But they won't.' Too angry to make sense, she tore on. 'Because you won't. Because I won't let you.'

She grabbed her handbag, belted her coat, and was into the hall before she knew what she was doing. She turned at the front door, and saw him in the doorway of the room she had just left. The roll of plans was still under his arm, and sardonic amusement was in every line of that devilish, handsome face.

'You'll hear from me,' she told him through gritted teeth.

Once out of the door, she was careful to close it quietly, to show how fully she was in command. At least she'd managed the last word this time.

The thought was little comfort as she walked through the village. The nerve of the man, to thrust himself into this contented community, and try and alter its whole way of life. But he wouldn't get away with it. She'd rally the Parish Council, the Women's Institute, the Church Tower Committee. On Monday, she'd visit County Planning.

She was so preoccupied, she almost walked right past her battered old Mini. And when she turned back to unlock it, there he was, just passing the war memorial and striding towards her with sinister speed.

'Your poppies.' He thrust the tray at her.

She knew she should have thanked him, but the common politeness stuck in her throat. She grabbed the tray and thrust it across the car to the passenger seat.

'I did call out,' he went on in a tone of distant interest. 'You didn't seem to hear. I suppose you had things on your mind.'

She slammed into the Mini and drove away without replying. Only when the car was toiling up the second hill for home did she realise that, once more, he'd managed to rob her of the last word.

CHAPTER FOUR

'SHE'S fine now, except for the sprained knee.' Far away in her sister's Edinburgh home, Meg's telephone voice was cheerful. 'It hasn't harmed the baby.'

'Thank goodness for that.'

Helen held the receiver gingerly, touching it only where she had to. Her fingers were leaving black marks on it, and probably on her face, too, and on the blue kerchief she'd wrapped round her hair. When this call had finally come after a morning of suspense, she'd taken it at once—no question of letting it ring while she washed the soot off her hands.

'I suppose,' she went on, 'you'll stay with her till Angus gets his next spell of leave from the oil rig?'

'At least a fortnight,' Meg confirmed. 'I can't leave her alone like this, with only four weeks to go.'

'Of course not.'

Nora hadn't made her usual Saturday call this morning. Instead, frighteningly early, a neighbour had rung to tell how she'd fallen and been taken to hospital, where they were keeping her for observation. Meg had packed a suitcase at breathless speed while Helen got the car going, and they'd arrived in Linford just as the bus had left for Edinburgh.

'I rang Mr Milburn at his home number, as you asked,' Helen told her mother. 'He was very nice about it. He's sure the part-timer can fill in while you're away.'

'She'll be glad of the extra money for Christmas.' Meg left an awkward pause. 'You told Will I couldn't make lunch?'

Grudgingly, Helen had. Three weeks ago, when she'd learnt how he'd sold Cuddymoor to Mike Armstrong, she'd declared she'd never speak to Will Purvis again. However, Meg had kept up the neighbourly habit of walking over to Pele Farm with a basket of shopping for a shared Saturday lunch, so Helen had been forced to see Will this morning and tell him what had happened.

'How did he take it?'

Helen passed on Will's regrets and good wishes, and added quickly, 'I only stayed a minute.'

'Oh. Yes. How's your cake getting on?'

'Er...' Helen glared at her sooty hands.

'So,' Meg might have seen the glare, 'the stove went out.'

'How did you——?' Helen stopped, exasperated at having given herself away so easily. 'I wasn't going to tell you.'

'I remembered on the journey. We were in such a hurry this morning, we forgot to put any coal on.'

'I didn't when I got back, either,' Helen admitted. She simply hadn't thought of it. Looking after the stove was her mother's job, and, as soon as she'd reached home, she'd kept loneliness at bay by tearing into her own weekly clean-round.

The upper rooms finished, she'd returned to the kitchen warmed by the exercise, and had set about the daily chores. She'd even fetched a few winter-bronzed hydrangeas from the garden, and had arranged them on the too-empty table before she'd eaten her salad, and cleared away, and washed up.

Then she had gone to the stove. Her first two attempts had used up the last of the wax and paraffin firelighters. Forced to try paper and sticks, she'd swept out every scrap of ash, and had collected the cinders for use when the fire was re-lit. If it ever was re-lit.

'At any rate, I've cleaned it,' she told her mother. 'It must be the cleanest stove this side of the Tweed.'

'And the coldest?'

'I'll soon get it going, don't worry.'

'Hm. Listen, chick, I've got to go.'

Helen blinked at the sudden use of that childhood nickname. 'All right. Give my love to Nora.'

The kitchen felt horribly empty when she put down the phone. Even on a fine Saturday afternoon there mightn't be anyone for miles. This was the first time she'd ever been alone here, she realised, and she certainly wasn't going to sit still and recall how Mike Armstrong had seen it coming, and had warned her.

She attacked the stove with renewed vigour. Oh, yes, if you could only light a stove with vigour, she thought bitterly half an hour later, she'd have succeeded long since. But you couldn't, and it simply wouldn't be coaxed.

She'd just have to use the electric oven, and bother the bills. Refusing to think how chilly the place was growing, she washed her hands and fetched her cake in its tin from the pantry. Thank goodness she'd mixed it last night, before everything had started going wrong.

When her mother rang again, she answered with surprise and pleasure. 'Did you forget something?'

'No, but I've organised something.' Meg sounded —could it be amused? Evasive? 'You've a visitor coming.'

'If you're sending Will Purvis over to help with the stove, forget it,' Helen snapped. 'I'd sooner freeze.'

'It isn't Will, and it isn't just the stove.'

'Who else, then?' Helen refused to be soothed. 'I don't care to see anyone from the village, after the way they're letting Mike Armstrong——'

'He asked me to give him time to reach the house, before I told you.'

'Who did?' Helen demanded, even more suspicious.

'It's incredibly kind of him. How lucky I knew the Moor Cottage phone number——'

'Did you say Moor Cottage?' Helen interrupted in outrage. 'Have you actually given Mike Armstrong an excuse to——?'

She broke off to the penetrating buzz from the bell-panel. Two short, one long, two short, which meant that whoever was pressing the button at the front door had been told the code.

'There he is,' Meg said, and broke the connection.

Helen glared at the burring phone. How could her mother invite that man up here, knowing how she felt about him? Knowing what he was doing to their village?

But that was just it. Meg, like all the others, refused to see the harm of his schemes. Helen had been to every house, and everywhere had found apathy or, worse, a positive welcome for his wretched hotel. So nobody but herself opposed him, and it looked very much as if he would get his planning permission. She'd warned them, but they wouldn't heed, and very soon—she shuddered to think of it—the bulldozers would be tearing up Cuddymoor.

Well, maybe she couldn't stop him there, but she could keep him out of here. She wouldn't answer that bell, not if he turned blue ringing it. She banged down the phone, marched to her rocking-chair, and prepared to sit out the next buzz.

It never came. The wind sighed in the valley, wood creaked in a cupboard, the tap dripped plok, plok, plok into the sink, but not a sound from the bell-panel. The tiny tick of her watch bustled time away. Five whole minutes, and still no buzz.

He must have gone. She hadn't heard his car depart, but then she hadn't heard it arrive either—the wind was in the wrong quarter. He'd gone without ringing again. He'd honoured the letter of whatever agreement he'd made with her mother, but this was what his promises were worth—one ring and away. He could now say he'd tried, and get on with some new, important scheme for devastating the countryside.

Struggling with a disappointment she wouldn't admit, she stood up. Only to check the front-door bolts and chains, she told herself as she made her way across the great hall. And, seeing that the sun had come from behind the clouds, she'd just look out and breathe the fresh air.

'Hi.' The tall, booted figure on the porch greeted her with an infuriating lack of surprise.

She whipped away her kerchief. Seemingly of its own accord, her hand fluffed and tidied her hair until she stopped it with a conscious effort, cramming the kerchief into the pockets of her blue-flowered overall.

'If you think I need——'

'Hang on.' He stared at the glorious gold hunter watch in his hand, then clicked the watch shut and tucked it into a pocket, its chain a gleaming line to the nearest button. 'Your mother said you wouldn't hold out for ten minutes.'

'And you thought I would?'

'I bet her you wouldn't answer at all. I lose.'

'Oh, you...you...'

She stammered to a halt. All through this time-wasting exchange she'd been trying not to see the dog sitting at his feet. Now he was speaking to it.

'Stand, Betsy.'

The dog stood, and Helen was lost, as she'd known she would be. One of Betsy's forebears might have been a Labrador, another a spaniel. Glossy black hair curled round her longish ears and sturdy frame; her massive chest and big feet were speckled white. She stared up with loving patience, and nothing could have kept Helen from stooping to stroke her rounded, gentle head.

Betsy looked up at Mike. When he confirmed that she might accept the caress, she sniffed Helen's ear.

'That's right, say hello to your new missis.'

Helen was so revelling in the clean doggy smell, the soft doggy fur, it was a moment before she understood. Even when she did, she had trouble dragging herself upright.

'She's beautiful. Gorgeous. But . . . we can't have a dog.'

'You can, you know.' He offered Betsy's lead.

'We can't.' Longing to accept, she took a step backwards. 'For one thing, we're both at work all day.'

'Meg and I each had a different solution to that one.'

Helen bitterly resented his easy use of her mother's name. The idea of them talking and planning for her was almost unbearable, yet here was their plan in person. Beautiful, darling Betsy. How could she be angry about that?

'She's big, she needs exercise,' he went on. 'Meg said you'd take her out in your lunch-hour.'

'Oh, wouldn't I just!'

'But if that's ever inconvenient, you can leave her at Pele Farm during the day.'

'Thanks.' Helen flung her head back. 'I don't need help from Will Purvis.'

'That's exactly what Meg guessed you'd say. But whatever you have against Will,' his wicked, devil's grin flashed for a moment, 'the offer's there. Sit, Betsy.'

Silently and without fuss, Betsy sat at Helen's feet.

With all that silky warmth nestled against her, Helen found it hard to bear grudges. How much nicer to dwell instead on the impossible, too-good-to-be-true idea that she and Betsy might have a future together.

'I'd love walking by the river in my lunch-hour. But Mike...' In her excitement she unthinkingly used his first name, and it didn't seem important. 'How can I ask any dog to sit with me through a working day?'

'Betsy will. She's a failed police dog.'

'Failed? Darling!' Helen had to stroke Betsy again, to make up for the awful idea. 'Did the nasty policemen think you weren't good enough, then?'

'They aren't nasty,' he told her from above. 'The handlers bring up the dogs in their own homes, with their own families.'

'And then they go and fail them?'

'It's no disgrace. She was a bit too playful, that's all.'

'What's wrong with playing a bit? It'll make her all the more fun to walk——' Helen broke off, confused to hear herself speaking as Betsy's owner.

'And don't get the idea that failed police dogs are ten a penny, either,' he went on. 'I've been two years on the waiting list.'

'Two years?' She rose to face him in bewilderment. 'You didn't even know me then.'

'That was for myself. They make great pets.'

'And you're offering her to me?' Helen couldn't keep the awed surprise from her voice. 'After a two-year wait?'

'Meg tells me you're up here on your own.'

'She'd no business to...' But Helen couldn't go on. Her resentment was almost gone, vanished in respect for this sacrifice he was willing to make.

'We agreed you could do with the—er—the company.'

She nodded, acknowledging the sense and the kindness. Only, what had her mother been thinking of? Dear old Boxer had died years ago; she'd always longed for another dog, and always known they couldn't keep one.

'The proper food——' she began, and closed her mouth tight. She had almost, to this outsider, used the word 'cost.'

And he understood it anyway. 'I've opened an account with the Grey Street pet shop.'

'Thanks, but...' she trailed off.

He proffered the dog-lead once more. Feeling wretchedly ungracious, she fought to keep her hands at her sides, to stop them taking it and making Betsy her own.

'We stay within our means,' she explained, half-ashamed. 'What we can't afford, we don't have.'

His voice hardened. 'We're back to the Thorntons, are we?'

'No... Yes... Don't hold it against me, Mike. It's a decent enough rule to live by.'

When had the sun gone into this latest bank of clouds? The wind had risen, too, with a keener edge to it. Slowly, he dropped the hand which held the lead.

'You're right, I shouldn't knock it.' He turned away. 'Here, Betsy.'

The dog moved to his side. Helen felt the chill at her feet where Betsy had been, and somewhere within her another chill, harder to define. 'You'll tell my mother?'

He nodded. 'She'd have liked to think of you with Betsy for company. And so would I.'

Helen stared at him. He'd spoken with such quiet sincerity. He was serious, as serious as when he'd agreed that staying within your income was a decent rule to live by.

'Do I need to remind you how very alone you are up here?' He meant it, all right. 'Betsy's trained to pin down and hold any intruder. Till you get to a phone, for instance.'

Against her will, Helen shuddered.

'I've heard,' he continued, 'about that boy who broke in here last year.'

'He was only fifteen, truanting. It...could have been very much worse.'

And next time, it might be. Knowing his mind as clear as her own, she waited for him to say it. And waited. And finally realised he wasn't going to.

Instead, he sighed. 'You know, I really thought I'd got it right this time.'

'Y-you did,' she hastened to assure him. 'It's only——'

'Those long walks you enjoy so much. Haven't you ever wanted a dog along on them?'

'Often!' she burst out passionately. 'A walk's a different thing again, with a dog.' She paused, yielding at last to the possibility. 'Maybe, after all, we could economise somewhere.'

'Your mother talked about a rise in salary you should have asked for six months ago.'

'Did she, indeed?'

Helen bristled, but saw the connection. With the extra money, she could certainly feed Betsy. And walk her, and love her, and talk to her through the long dark evenings until Meg came back. What was more, being able to mention a new mouth to feed —a guard dog—would be a very good way of opening negotiations for that long-overdue raise.

'Can I ... can I change my mind?' She held out her hand.

He put the leather loop in her palm and closed her fingers on it. He only meant to make it hers— he couldn't possibly have guessed at the bright, sweet surge of her blood as her hand lay cradled in both of his, warmly held, guarded, safe.

Safe? Why, he was about as safe as an open power-point. Clutching the dog-lead, she jerked her hand away at the same moment he dropped his.

'Your...' He cleared his throat, and started again. 'Your mother will be pleased. And so will I,' his tone steadied, 'to think of you and Betsy looking after each other.'

Still light-headed, she stared at him suspiciously. 'You haven't got her electronically bugged, I suppose?'

His shout of laughter echoed from the old stone pillars. 'Have you been seeing too many James Bond movies?'

'Oh, dear.' She shook her head to clear it. 'What a stupid thing to say.'

'You've just invented a new weapon in the planning war.'

'Worse than stupid.' As the pounding of her heart quietened, she found it easier to make sense. 'Ungrateful.'

'Oh, gratitude.' He turned away, dismissing the word.

'Don't go.' She put out a hand to detain him, and dropped it just in time. 'I've ... I've got to say it properly.'

He waited. 'I'm only fetching her things. What do you want to say properly?'

'That ...' She swallowed. 'That I really do appreciate your giving me Betsy, and I'll always look after her as she deserves.' There, it was out. Even if it did sound like a little girl's thank-you letter.

'My pleasure,' he responded formally, and moved to the back of the estate car drawn up against the rhododendrons.

Still embarrassed by her own stilted primness, she asked, 'What things of hers have you brought?'

'Basket.' He opened the rear door. 'Blanket.' He lifted its neat folds, checking. 'Bowl. And a week's supply of the kind of food she's used to.' Laden, he rejoined her on the porch. 'I'll carry this stuff down. Forgive me, but I'll have to stay long enough to make sure she's settling.'

'F-forgive you?'

Had she really been so unwelcoming that he felt he must apologise for his own thoughtful kindness? To make up for it she opened the door wide, and led them all across the great hall.

'A two-year wait!' she marvelled as she ushered them through the green baize door. 'That's a thing money couldn't buy.'

Released into the kitchen, Betsy looked up and waited. Mike put down the basket, spread it with the blanket, and gave Helen several sheets of typescript. 'These are the orders she's been trained to.'

Helen scanned them, and used the one that seemed to fit. Sure enough, Betsy relaxed and began a quiet inspection of her new quarters, following her shiny black nose from window to sink to pantry door.

'Not there, darling.' Helen hastened to guard her from the stove. 'It's hot. At least, it should be——'

She broke off with a start. Turning from the dog, she had found Mike Armstrong much nearer than she'd expected. Near enough to raise a hand, and run a finger from her eyebrows to the roots of her hair.

'Did you know,' he showed her his black finger-tip, 'how much soot you've got on you?'

'Is . . . is it very bad?' She dabbed at her brow. 'There didn't seem much point in washing, till I'd got the stove going.'

'Would you let me do that?'

She wrestled with the temptation. This, she knew, was one of the reasons he'd come. The reason her mother had called him in the first place. It must be because of that call, because he'd learnt she was alone up here, that he'd decided to make her the precious gift of Betsy—but how could she accept yet more favours from him?

'I shouldn't let it get the better of me,' she objected. 'I've got to learn how to manage it, now my mother isn't here.'

'Sure.' He knelt to inspect her efforts. 'But how often will you be needing to light it?'

'Not at all,' she admitted with heartfelt resolve. 'We don't generally. . . What's so funny?'

'Nothing.' But as he looked at her rolled paper, crossed sticks, and balanced pieces of coal, his lips twitched again. 'Off you go, then,' he went on, as if it were all settled.

He had this habit, she remembered in the bathroom, of making obedience seem the only sensible course.

When she saw herself in the glass, she could only marvel at his self-control. Her eyebrows crackled with soot, and the only white on her forehead was where he'd touched her. Yet he hadn't cracked a smile when she'd answered the door in this state. No wonder he'd wanted to laugh at her pathetic efforts with the stove. They must have been simply the last straw.

She returned to the kitchen shining clean, with her hair bouncy from brushing. She'd taken off her overall, too, and put on the becoming blue sweater which had just happened to be at hand in her bedroom.

When she saw the flames leaping in the stove, she couldn't believe it. Sure enough, though, they danced round a solid coal heart already glowing at the centre. Which it would continue to do, she promised herself, from now on.

'Th-thank you.' She cleared her throat, and raised her voice to be heard at the sink where he was washing his hands. 'Thank you very much indeed.'

'It was a pleasure. I take it,' he gestured at the cake, 'you want to bake that?'

She nodded. 'I'll start it as soon as the oven's hot.'

'Shall we run Betsy while you're waiting? To get her comfortable with you?'

Helen had her coat on before he'd finished speaking.

Betsy loved the Lin. She splashed through the shallows, paddled strongly to the middle, and returned with a shining wet stick which they then had to throw in for her again and again. While she swam and splashed, Helen showed Mike the squirrel hoard she had lately discovered, and the tree where once, when she was little, a tawny owl had raised its family.

'My father and I watched for hours, from a brushwood hide we made. But that's long gone,' she sighed, 'the way everything goes.'

'Not quite everything.'

'How can you say that, when——?'

But she couldn't quarrel with him. Not here, where the river murmured and the trees made lacy patterns against the fitful winter sunlight. Not now, when Betsy had just brought the stick to her like a present. Helen took it to throw again, but Betsy had finished her game. Water flew from her as she shook herself dry, and, without needing to discuss it, they all turned up the hill for home.

In the darkening kitchen garden, Helen surveyed the tangled raspberry canes and overgrown beds. 'You should have seen this when my father was looking after it.'

Mike closed the gate, and stood back to let her lock it. 'You still miss him, don't you?'

'I suppose I do. He was a friend...' She swallowed hard, and turned the big old key.

'How old were you—eleven?' His voice was low.

She drew the key out, and felt it suddenly heavy, cold, dead in her hand. 'It was a long time ago.'

'But you're still——'

'I am not! I had to grow up fast, after——'

'Still mourning him.' The deep voice silenced her.

She managed to look up at last. The dark eyes met hers steadily in the gathering dusk, and something in his stillness, his attentiveness, made it easy to try and explain her outburst.

'Derek...this man I knew...well, he said I'd never properly...' But she couldn't repeat it after all.

Mike completed it for her. 'Never properly grown up?'

'It isn't true,' she flashed again, reliving the whole miserable argument as she stared across at the old stone wall where it had come to a head. 'I'm as grown up as he is.'

'You probably are.' Mike touched her elbow, the briefest signal to start them along the path. 'We're none of us as mature as we think.'

'Derek certainly isn't.'

The wall was soft now with winter twilight. On that Sunday afternoon last August, it had been soaking up the sun for hours. It had given out a drowsy heat which had spread through them, her and Derek, as they'd relaxed on a blanket he'd fetched from his car. In the sleepy, sheltered privacy, she'd accepted his caresses, returned them even, until they had frightened her with their urgency and depth. That was when she'd wanted to say no, and he hadn't let her, and it had ended in painful absurdity.

'The fuss he made about that bee sting!' She kicked at a stone. 'And, whatever he said, it wasn't my fault.'

She heard Mike's little snort of laughter, and turned an indignant stare on him. In a moment, however, she was smiling with him. Suddenly, the memory lost its power to hurt.

'I suppose,' she admitted for the first time, 'I shouldn't have expected him to wait till the bee unwound its sting.'

'Not everybody can do that,' Mike agreed, and waited for her to unlock the back door.

She went before him into the passage and switched on the light. A brief word released Betsy, who padded ahead of them into the kitchen while Helen slipped out of her coat. As Mike took it from her shoulders and draped it on its hanger, she turned her face up to him in appeal.

'He said it was my thrashing about that disturbed the bee. But if he'd only left me alone——'

She broke off, conscious of having given away more than she meant to. She glanced up at Mike, but his eyes were hooded, his smile a trifle grim as he hung his own jacket beside hers.

'He wasn't the man for you.'

'That's not how he put it. What he said was...'

But she couldn't repeat it. Glad to be busy, she kicked off her wellington boots, placed them neatly side by side, and stepped into her lighter shoes.

It was Mike who finished the idea for her, with matter-of-fact confidence. 'He said you didn't like men at all.'

She raised her head so fast, her hair bounced on her shoulders. 'How did you know that?'

'It's a standard when a woman doesn't fancy you.'

'I bet *you* never...'

But she had to stop again, embarrassed at what she'd been about to say. She couldn't imagine Mike Armstrong using that explanation—but then, she knew, in some way she refused to think about, that he'd never need to.

'Did he call you frigid?'

She stared up at him, her spirits rising.

'And threaten you'd die an old maid?'

She nodded. 'A...' She nerved herself, and faced the word triumphantly. 'A *frigid* old maid.'

He laughed. 'That came out as if you needed to say it.'

'I don't, any more.'

'It's not a thing you should ever have worried about.' His eyes held hers. 'Because you aren't.'

It was as if he'd deliberately entered her mind. As if he'd used some magic of his own to conjure the memory of that soft night beyond the porch, the heathery scent as he'd folded her in his arms, the hardness of his mouth possessing hers.

He'd let her go the minute she'd resisted, but she hadn't wanted him to. She'd wanted him to go on, to go further, to lead her into that tingling inner world where sensuality was all. Her inner self had leapt to the bounds of her being that night, and had demanded to be joined, and made double, and made whole.

A light, doggy patter on the tiles brought a welcome distraction. Betsy stood looking up at them, patient but enquiring, as if she wondered what was taking them so long.

Helen spoke to her with relief. 'You want your supper, don't you, darling? You shall have it, the minute I've started my cake.'

She darted to the stove. Finding it exactly right, she switched on the light over the table, and waited there for Mike and Betsy to join her. Putting a cake in the oven, especially a Christmas cake, was something of a ceremony, and must have the full attention of everyone present.

He took it as seriously as she could have wished. When she brought the cake over from the table he was at the stove before her, opening the oven door wide. While she slid it on to its shelf, he drew that gleaming hunter watch from his pocket, snapped it open, and compared it with the wall-clock.

'How long do you give it?'

'Four hours.' She stood back to let him close the door.

'So you're here for the evening?'

She had to admit it. She generally managed to be out on a Saturday night, if only to a whist drive, or amateur dramatics, or a meal with a woman friend. However, he didn't seem to notice her shame.

'I'm glad of that. Seeing we still have to settle Betsy.'

'W-we?'

'I'm more than sure she's going to be very happy, here with you,' he told her gently. 'But I can't go till I know, can I?'

'I s-suppose not. How...how long can you stay?'

'As long as it takes.' He glanced at where the dog was inspecting her basket beside the dresser. 'Is that where you want it, by the way?'

'Absolutely. She can have it there in the daytime, and at night I'll take it to my room——'

Helen broke off, feeling the beginning of that wretched, give-away blush. And yet why shouldn't she speak of her bedroom? she asked herself impatiently. Most people had one.

'If you haven't any other plans,' she went on fast, to cover her awkwardness, 'perhaps you'd let me give you some supper?'

Why did his smile make her feel so good? Was it the slight unevenness of the white teeth tempering the dark, strong features with sudden humanity? Or could it be the warmth of understanding in the dark eyes? She looked away hastily. 'I know it's early...'

'Early or not, I'm famished. What are we having?'

CHAPTER FIVE

A MAN in the house again. Meg's wistful comment of five weeks ago came back to Helen with new meaning as she bustled happily to the fridge. Had it really only taken a morning alone, and trouble with the stove, to change her feelings like this? Or was the change less sudden than she was prepared to believe?

She put the question aside in the delightful business of choosing supper. He was hungry, so it had to be substantial—and quick.

'Liver and bacon.' She pounced on both triumphantly. 'Mushrooms, onions, tomatoes, jacket potatoes——'

'Stop!' he cried in mock anguish. 'How am I to survive until those are baked?'

'I'll put them in the hotter oven, right away.'

She did, scrubbed and skewered to cook faster. When she had done this, she found that he had mixed Betsy's supper and was ready to pass the bowl across to her.

'You have to be the one to feed her.'

'To help us make friends,' she agreed, and set the bowl in the place she had already chosen, beyond the pantry door.

Well-trained Betsy would never eat without her special password. On hearing it from her new mistress, she cleared the bowl in minutes and settled into her basket with a satisfied air.

Helen, too, felt satisfied. As if to make up for her troubles earlier today, her cooking now went exactly to plan. The big pan sizzled on the stove, and food waited to be put into it, in due order, as soon as the potatoes signalled their mealy savour from the oven. She set two places cornerwise at the big table, and, on hearing that Mike liked green vegetables, sent him to the pantry for the curly Celtic she'd bought in Linford market.

He handed it over, then held up a half-ground, perfumed kernel. 'I found this all by itself on the lower shelf.'

'It belongs in the jar on the dresser,' she told him, intent on her timing. 'I grated it into the cake last night, then put it away in the wrong place.'

'You always add nutmeg to your Christmas cake?'

'It's my own special extra.'

'For Bridget.' That smile hovered again at the wide, tender mouth.

Tender? Since when could such a word describe Mike Armstrong and his goings-on? She hastily brought her attention back to their supper, and forgot her uncomfortable thoughts in the pleasure of getting everything right.

And she did. The deep brown liver and crinkled bacon all parted like butter to the knife. As for the vegetables, green, scarlet, pale brown and fluffy white, they were perfect even by her own exacting standards.

'That,' he put down his knife and fork on his empty plate, 'is the kind of supper the angels eat in heaven.'

'So you're an authority on heaven?' she teased.

'I am.' In the soft glow from the pull-down light, his mouth settled in a sombre line. 'Or as much as I had of it.'

'We're talking about Celia again, aren't we?' Helen asked with sudden, complete conviction. 'Was she your wife?'

He shook his head. 'Cele wasn't made to be a wife. She went nursing, in Africa.'

'I see.' Helen fought a wave of the same misery as had hit her when she'd first heard of this high-minded woman he had loved.

'I visited her, saw her working.' He tensed, as if in remembered pain. 'It brought her alive in a way I never could.'

'So you don't think she'll be back?' Helen asked, wondering why she should suddenly feel so light-hearted.

He shook his head vigorously, almost as if he were shaking off the past. 'There are other women.'

She jerked round to look at him. Of course he'd have found other women, and they'd have found him. She'd have to accept that, she realised, even as she tried to tell herself that it was of no interest to her either way.

'Right here, for instance,' he went on in a caressing murmur. 'A border princess.'

His knee touched hers, and she jumped up with a great show of briskness. 'So, which am I? A border princess, or a half-drowned ginger cat?'

'Both.' He smiled as he stood up to join her.

She set about clearing the table. 'I don't like doing this while a guest's here, but with everything in the one room . . .'

'We'll soon have it finished.' And he was right—
the washing-up was done almost before she realised
they'd started it.

'So, Betsy's settled.' He hung the towel on its
usual hook. 'And you've fed me like a chieftain.
Shall I be on my way?'

She wiped out the orange bowl. 'That's up to
you.'

'Is it? You really mean that?'

She nodded, not looking at him.

'Right.' He moved to the sitting-corner, and
settled in a rocking-chair. 'Then I wait to see the
cake come out.'

She answered as calmly as possible, 'That'll be
a good couple of hours yet.'

But she almost floated to join him in the other
chair. She switched on the rose-shaded standard
lamp, and Betsy blinked awake. Helen smoothed
the dog's ears, marvelling at how everything had
changed in a few short hours.

'I don't think I'll ever stop being grateful for her,'
she said as Betsy settled again. 'Now, could we go
through this list of words they've taught her?'

She soon mastered them, and was content to relax
with pleasant, neutral topics. They spoke of earlier
Thorntons, plain farmers until younger son Adam
made his sugar fortune in the late eighteenth
century. Of Mike's great-grandfather, who in his
day had beaten all comers at Northumbrian wres-
tling, and had won the gold hunter watch his great-
grandson now used with such reverence.

Presently, in a hush of warm baking smells,
wearing her best oven-mitts, Helen carried the cake
to the table. Then she made them wait ten solemn

minutes by the gold hunter until, tongue between teeth, she stripped off the greaseproof paper. And there it stood, deep gold, smoothly rounded, a triumph of a Christmas cake.

She gave him a sideways look. 'It's all right, isn't it?' she asked, as casually as she could.

'Very all right.' But he wasn't looking at the cake.

That was the moment when everything came together. The unexpected pleasures of the day—the walk, the meal, the quiet evening—all seemed to have been carrying her forward to this. Before she knew it her arms were round his neck, her lips offered, to be locked with his in a harmony that felt so right, so perfect, it might have been intended since time began.

So good, and yet so clearly only a beginning. She pressed nearer, and the world took fire.

They strained to each other, mouths mingling and exploring. Her fingers traced his earlobe, his neck, the smooth hair at his nape, hovered at the edge of all the new territory they wanted to make their own. Her spine responded to his smoothing hands and she nestled closer, close enough to sense how easily their two bodies could have joined as one...

She dragged hurriedly free. Pushing at her hair with trembling hands, she wondered why she suddenly felt so cold, and so lonely. Was it fear that had entered her with that kiss? Or was it something else, something worse, a new desire which only he could quench?

'How...?' She steadied her voice. 'How did that happen?'

'These things do.' His eyes burnt into hers. 'Especially when a man wants a woman as I want you.'

She huddled back from him. 'I didn't know——'

'Oh, yes you did, my darling. You knew it when we first met in the storm.' But he spoke more easily, regaining control with a shaky laugh. 'I hate to think what your bees might have done to me that day.'

'Oh, but they'd never have stung *you*,' she said quickly, and refused to ask herself why she was so sure of that.

'They'd have done anything you ordered,' he told her, half-serious. 'Just like that storm you walked through as if you owned it.'

'Owned it?' She grabbed at the distraction, and tried to see herself as he had seen her. 'Was I really so arrogant?'

'Not arrogant, only very much at home. Which is fair enough,' he added with a glance round the old kitchen, 'seeing you were right in your own backyard.'

'I wouldn't call the moors anyone's backyard.'

'Call them what you like, they're where you belong.'

'That's not the same as owning them. If I did...' She stopped, brought up against the great question which separated them.

He tackled it at once, full on. 'I suppose the Thorntons used to own Cuddymoor?'

She nodded. 'I wish they still did.'

'And there it is.' He gave her a long, searching look. 'You'll never accept my plans for it, will you?'

'Never.'

He touched the curl falling over her brow. 'You always look as if you've a light inside.'

The heat of the tiny contact, almost painful, stung her with a thousand needles of desire. She took a step backwards, and he dropped his hand.

'I'd better go.'

He made for the door. Watching his tall, retreating figure, her sense of loss was so great, she could hardly stop herself calling his name aloud. She had taken a breath, parted her lips, half put out her hand, when he looked back over his shoulder.

'See me out?'

She couldn't answer; the words stuck in her throat. Yet her body moved of its own accord, followed him, put on her coat, took up her torch. Betsy woke and padded after them.

Mike stood aside, and Helen passed him. Careful not to touch him, trying hard not even to think of him, she kept ahead up the stairs and through the great hall. At the front door she found her voice at last, but only to murmur the command which brought Betsy to sit at her feet.

'I can see I don't need to worry about her.' Mike stooped to take his farewell of the dog. 'She's decided where she belongs.'

Helen looked down at the two of them. Once more she had to fight that wretched, engulfing sense of loss. For want of a word or a gesture, something infinitely worthwhile was slipping out of her reach. She didn't understand what it was, or how she could prevent it, but she must speak.

'Yes, Betsy's made up her mind.' Her voice sounded small, weak, unfamiliar in her ears. 'I take it you have, too?'

'About where I belong?' He left the dog and rose slowly to face her, an unreadable shadow with the moonlight behind him. 'You settled that for me weeks ago, when you decided I was an outsider.'

'Only because you're trying to change everything.'

'Change happens, whether you welcome it or not.'

'So I should accept it, like everybody else in this village? How convenient for you.'

'Dammit, Helen.' His voice was strained. 'I didn't want to start this again.'

She let out her breath, soft as the little wind rustling the leaves. 'It's still there.'

'I was hoping we might begin to work round it.'

'You think we could?' She was glad of the dark, to disguise her eagerness. 'Could we ever forget our differences?'

'We managed it tonight, for a while.'

She bent to caress the placid dog at her feet. 'I'll always be grateful to you for Betsy. And for lighting the stove.'

'I was glad to help. Really glad,' he went on, as if to show that it wasn't merely a form of words. 'It was nice being on the same side as you, Helen.'

Thus encouraged, brave in the obscurity of the porch, she lifted her head to face him. 'Why couldn't we talk like this back there in the house?'

'Because you're still afraid.'

'I'm not!' she denied hotly. 'Or at least——' She broke off, bewildered at the new idea. 'I trust you, Mike.'

'Then you shouldn't!' He spoke with such violence that Betsy shot to attention. 'I'm only a man, Helen. Don't ever forget that.'

'I'm not likely to.' She found she was trembling.

'And that's not the only reason we can't talk,' he added more quietly. 'There's the house itself. It's grabbed me and won't let go.'

She couldn't help her quick little gasp of surprise. She'd never put it into words before, but he'd described so exactly how she herself felt.

'What I could do here.' He swept an arm to where the row of windows shone in the moonlight. 'It could be as glorious as when Adam Thornton first built it.'

'I see you've remembered his name at last.'

'If ever a man deserved to be remembered, he does.'

She was impressed in spite of herself. 'Honestly?'

'That living-space of yours. What a superb kitchen it must have made.'

'It was known, in the county,' she murmured, pleased. 'Servants always stayed. All their lives, some of them.'

'Any staff would. Though I'd change a few things, just to take advantage of modern technology.'

'Like what?' she asked, suddenly on edge.

'Well, I'd add some worktops. And it stands to reason you'd want a more up-to-date stove——'

'You've been planning how you'd make the place over,' she cut in, disgusted. 'After coming here in friendship.'

He didn't answer, and her words died away among the hushed night-sounds. A distant car climbed the hill, changed gear, and hummed down into nothingness. A ghostly shape hovered for a moment above the rhododendrons and winged away, a barn owl in search of more profitable hunting.

'Well, you can forget it.' Closely followed by Betsy, she stepped inside the door and held it between them. 'This house is my birthright, and you're never getting your hands on it.'

'No,' he answered harshly. 'You'd rather let it rot.'

She gasped in fury. To speak as if she were neglecting the place, after all her hours of loving care! After all her mopping and mending, hammering and puttying, the worry, the loneliness—she had so much to say, she didn't know where to begin.

'Better a Thornton ruin, I suppose,' he turned on his heel, 'than a proper, lived-in home with somebody else's name on it.'

And then he'd gone, coiled into his car and closing its door before she could find an answer. The engine purred to life, the headlights swept the drive, and as it glided to the gates she realised that, once more, he'd had the last word.

There was nothing to do but bolt the door and put up the chain. She leant against it in the darkness, hands to her burning cheeks, eyes following the lights of his car until they passed the gateway and disappeared, and only the moon shone through the curtainless windows.

'I hate him,' she breathed. 'Hate him!'

Yet her own face felt disappointingly smooth under her hands. Her fingers ached with memories of another cheek, another jaw, firm and just a little bristled. And when she moved through the moonlight, a faithful patter followed at her heels. How could she hate the man who had given her Betsy?

She let them through the door in the panelling, closed it, and jerked up her head. What was that in the air? Up here it was no more than a hint, but as she hurried down the stairs it grew ever fuller.

'It can't be.' She paused at the foot of the stairs. Betsy's sensitive black nose quivered.

'It isn't,' Helen told her with determination. 'We're both imagining it.'

But it was. It hit her the moment she opened the kitchen door, and grew in strength as she crossed to the table. Too agitated to think of putting away her coat, she stood over the cake on its wire tray.

'This is where it's coming from.'

She breathed up the ghosts of butter, and dried fruit, and lemon peel. Trying to keep them with her, she made for her chair and breathed again, rocking gently back and forth through the waves of this other fragrance she could no longer deny.

The scent of nutmeg.

'So what are you trying to tell me, Bridget?'

Betsy came to lay her head on Helen's lap. Helen smoothed the silky ears, and looked down into the wide brown eyes.

'I don't believe it,' she said firmly.

All right, so she'd kissed him. He'd been kind—more than kind—and she'd been grateful. But he was a businessman, a dealer, one who gave only in order to take. Seeking his left-handed bargain, just like the devil she'd first taken him for.

'You're wrong, Bridget.' She picked up the dog-basket to carry to her room, and paused. 'What's one evening,' she demanded of the scented air, 'in a whole lifetime?'

Bridget seemed unimpressed. The scent of nutmeg wafted everywhere in the house during the next few days, until Helen, still arguing, learnt to live with it.

'What does Bridget know about it, anyway?' she observed to Betsy. 'A hundred and fifty years away from us all.'

Betsy perked her floppy ears and waved her plumy tail; she was a dear companion in the general emptiness. Not that Helen allowed herself to think of her home, or her life, as empty.

'I'm fine,' she told Mr Milburn when he visited her at work the following week. 'How's your office without my mother?'

'Limping along,' he joked, a round, solid man who looked like a sixty-year-old badger. 'My wife worries about you, though, alone in that great place.'

'She needn't,' Helen said quickly. 'Though it's kind of her,' she added, humbled by such concern from people who weren't even Linrother neighbours. 'But I'm managing very well.'

'Good, good. I said you would, an independent little thing like you.' Mr Milburn nodded in satisfaction. 'But you'll come to the party, just the same?'

'What party?'

'Haven't I given you the invitation?' He clicked his tongue in self-reprimand, and handed her the thick white envelope he had been carrying. 'Friday at eight, buffet. For the space.'

'The...' Helen took out the formal, engraved invitation.

'And bring Betsy, of course.' Already he was preparing to leave. 'We'll put her with my daughter's two——'

'Charlotte's staying, then?'

'Everybody's staying,' he told her expansively, 'to see the space.'

'And her dogs...?'

'Quiet as lambs. Betsy'll be fine with them, and you'll be able to look in on her.'

'It says RSVP,' Helen called as he made for the door.

'But you have, haven't you?' He inclined his broad badger-head. 'You can come?'

'Well—er—thanks,' Helen began, and as the idea grew on her, 'thanks a lot. I'll look forward to it.'

She'd been to Milburn parties before with her mother, and hadn't found them very exciting. Still, it was a chance for an outing. And to dress up, she decided, as she piled her new-washed hair to the top of her head in a fluffed-out, red-gold crown, and smoothed the narrow skirt of her beloved midnight-blue dress.

'You look charming, my dear.' In the wide entrance hall of her Victorian home, white-haired Mrs

Milburn patted her own ample, black velvet curves. 'I'd never have believed a waist could be so tiny.'

'Er—thanks.' Helen nodded to the maid who had let her in, and held up Betsy's basket. 'Er—where does this go?'

'Right here.'

The side-room appeared to be a study. Beyond the bright circle of the desk-lamp, two black Labradors left their cushions to acknowledge the visitors politely. Helen chose a place a little way from them, by the two-seater chesterfield, and settled Betsy down.

'Now you're not to worry, she'll be fine.' Mrs Milburn, a practised hostess, moved her guest back to the hall. 'You'll find George in the drawing-room, showing off the new conservatory.'

'A conservatory?' Helen repeated, always interested in house improvements.

'Do go and see it. We're very pleased.'

Mrs Milburn turned to the next arrivals, and Helen followed the quiet, continuous burr of voices. Guests stood in groups about the soft-lit, deep-carpeted room with its English landscape paintings, its chintzy armchairs pushed against the wall, its walnut-inlaid cupboards and mahogany side-tables. Helen could see Charlotte Milburn, long-legged in skimpy gold, supervising some mixing process at the white-covered bar. Beyond her, the handsome room now opened triumphantly to a new structure of white wrought-iron and glass.

The conservatory certainly was worth celebrating. Queen Victoria herself might have admired it—a series of gleaming, exuberant curves light as a bubble, yet defying the late-November chill with a leafy, flowery warmth.

'Double-glazed and centrally heated, do you see?' George Milburn hurried out of it to greet Helen's arrival. 'But all absolutely traditional.'

'It's super,' Helen agreed, lulled by the crackling glow of the applewood fire.

Those marble garlands and swags of fruit round the fireplace must have been horrors to clean, yet they shone. Every niche and awkward crevice had been wiped clear, just as they had on the moulded ceiling. If only she could spend this kind of time and money on Thornton Pele!

But she couldn't allow herself to go on feeling such envy. When a white-coated waiter presented his tray she gladly took a glass and raised it.

'To the space,' Mr Milburn pledged. 'Can't be doing with that word conservatory—it takes too long to say.'

'The space.' Helen tasted the dancing pale-gold liquid. 'Er—what is this?'

'Champagne cocktail.' He set his glass on the mantelpiece, next to a Wedgwood vase. 'Can't say I'm fond of it, but Charly thinks it helps a party along.'

'It's—er—very good,' Helen murmured.

She only pretended to drink again. With a seven-mile drive home, she wasn't sure she should be touching the drink at all, but at least she'd make it last the whole evening.

'We've havered and hovered about it for years.' George Milburn gazed contentedly across into the conservatory. 'Nothing seemed right, until he showed how we could keep the period style, and still use modern technology.'

Something about the phrase brought Helen's head up. '*Who* showed you that?'

'Why, Mike, of course. Who else could make such a good job of it? He'll be here any minute.' Mr Milburn surveyed the door. 'He's celebrating, too. Got his planning today, for that bit of scrubland your way—what's it called ...?'

'Cuddymoor.' Helen swallowed her drink in good earnest.

'That's it, that's it. Over here, Philip.' Mr Milburn summoned his partner. 'I see Sir Geoffrey's just arrived. Look after Helen, will you?'

Philip Harkness, tanned from a recent holiday and elegant in a dark red velvet jacket, was very willing. One or two of the other women were glancing his way, and his strikingly fair wife in her cyclamen-coloured dress looked unhappier than ever. At any other time Helen might have thought him altogether too willing. Just now, not thinking at all, she let him take her empty glass, and accepted a full one in return.

So her beloved childhood playground was 'that bit of scrubland', was it? And Mike Armstrong had his planning permission, and she'd been tricked into coming here to help him celebrate.

Well, not tricked exactly. Even in her present rage, she couldn't use that word of vague, beaming Mr Milburn. But it amounted to the same thing.

She'd leave at once. No, she couldn't do that, it would be too rude to hosts who'd invited her from pure kindness. Maybe in half an hour though, or an hour at the most...

'Good, aren't they?' Philip Harkness was once more taking her glass away. 'Here, have another.'

'Thanks.' The champagne shimmered on her palate, her tongue, her throat. 'So, how's the Caribbean at this season?' she asked from politeness, and never heard the answer.

He'd arrived. In the plainest of dinner-jackets, with white shirt and black bow-tie, his dark height still dominated the gathering. All heads turned to him, and the man George Milburn had called Sir Geoffrey greeted him as an old friend.

'That's how these things are done.' Helen drained her glass without tasting it. 'I suppose Sir Geoffrey's somebody important in County Planning.'

'No.' Philip Harkness seemed bewildered. 'He's... Where are you going?'

'The study, I suppose it is.' She spoke very carefully, to make up for this slight dizziness. 'You know. The little room off the other side of the entrance hall.'

'Oh, yes?' His eyes half closed, and the tip of his tongue suddenly showed between his teeth. 'Yes,' he went on, equally clear and careful, 'I know that room.'

She wondered if the champagne cocktail was fighting with his stomach as it seemed to be with hers. He had begun peering round the room in the oddest way, as if looking for something. Or as if he might need to make a sudden dash for the door, she decided, as he edged the two of them into a direct line towards it.

'And why there, might I ask?'

'I just thought I would,' she answered at random, staring absently into the very blue, half-closed eyes. 'I have to see a dog about a man,' she added, and laughed at her own wit.

He put their glasses on a passing tray. 'Any special man?'

'What's special about any man?'

She broke away from him, and dodged a white-coated waiter. She really couldn't face another of those fizzy drinks—the last had tasted like vinegar. She kept well clear of Mike Armstrong, and deliberately turned her back when she saw him watching her.

Mrs Milburn murmured something about supper as she passed. Helen nodded brightly, and murmured something back about Betsy.

The guests must be all here by now, for the hall was blessedly quiet. So was the study, where the Labradors opened their eyes and Betsy sat up in greeting. Helen flopped to the couch, and took comfort as she always did in her pet's silent friendship.

'All the wrong people have the power and the money.' She buried her fingers in the thick, doggy fur. 'But at least I've got you.'

Betsy snuggled up to her skirt, a calm, living centre in a room that was starting to spin.

It went on spinning, faster and faster, and actually seemed to tip sideways when the door softly opened. But it was only that she'd turned too quickly, Helen realised, hating the sudden wild hope which leapt through her, yet unable to deny it.

She needn't have been so eager. It was only Philip Harkness, hesitating by the closed door.

'I didn't realise we'd have company.'

'It's all right, they won't bother you.' She moved politely to make room for him on the couch. 'If you want to be quiet here for a while...'

'That's one way of putting it.' He lowered himself to her side. 'They've all gone to the dining-room for supper, but somehow I'm not hungry.'

'Me neither,' she agreed. 'In a little while, I'll——' She stopped and stared down in disbelief. 'Will you kindly take your hand off my knee?'

'Certainly.' He moved it smoothly up the line of her skirt to her waist. 'All in good time, eh?'

Before she could collect her senses he was smothering her in a greedy, open-mouthed kiss.

CHAPTER SIX

PHILIP wasn't taking Helen's resistance seriously, and no wonder. Quite apart from the muzziness in her head, her arms were pinned to her sides, and not only was her mouth out of action, but he was covering her nose, too. She couldn't breathe. She wanted to ask if he'd ever suffocated anybody this way, but couldn't utter so much as a squeak, however hard she tried.

Then she heard a brief, businesslike growl. She'd barely recognised it as Betsy's, when a furry body hurled itself across her, and doggy claws dug briefly into her lap.

But that was only incidental, she realised, gasping for air. It was her companion who was the target. Already Betsy had him pinned to the back of the couch, her paws on his shoulders, her teeth bared, absolutely still. It was that stillness which was so frightening, and such a clear warning.

And it had all been so quick. So quiet. Helen glanced at the two Labradors and found them still sleeping peacefully. They might wake any minute, though, and then goodness knew what would happen. Shuddering as she imagined the noise and excitement which could bring other people running in here, she gave the command which would call Betsy off.

Brisk, capable, and silent as ever, Betsy turned and jumped to the floor. Helen sensed her readiness for further action if it was needed, but at least the other two dogs hadn't stirred.

'Good lord!' Philip Harkness pulled an immaculate handkerchief from his top pocket, and wiped his brow. 'Does she always do that to your boyfriends?'

Revolted, Helen put a hand to her own spinning head. Before she could find a reply another voice, one whose deep tones she hardly recognised, cut in from the doorway.

'What the hell do you think you're up to?'

'Mike!'

Helen's heart leapt, stopped, leapt again. What must they look like? She turned back to her would-be lover with renewed disgust; his hair was tousled, his bow-tie standing on end, and his shirt gaped where a button had come off. And she must be equally messy herself. Her wide, frightened eyes, and Betsy crouching watchful at her feet, must tell the whole story.

'You tinpot Casanova!'

Mike's words came out jagged as broken glass. Helen thought she'd seen him angry before, but she hadn't known the half of it. Never had his dark eyes seemed so narrow and dangerous, his long mouth so clamped, his cleft chin so threatening. Watching his strong hands clench into fists, she jumped to her feet and choked out a protest.

'Mike, you can't!'

'Out of my way.' He'd already crossed the room, and thrust her aside with a sweep of his arm.

'I wouldn't, old man.' Philip Harkness stayed seated, trying for a casual note though his voice shook a little. 'I'm a solicitor, remember...'

Mike grabbed his lapels and dragged him to his feet. 'So sue me!'

He swung, and Helen closed her eyes. She still had to listen, though, to the horrible crack of fist against chin, and the muffled flop and the groan of springs as Philip Harkness dropped back to the couch. When she could bear to look again, he was still there, holding the side of his jaw.

'That's going to cost you.'

'Worth every penny. I'll enjoy telling the court why I did it, too.'

'M-Mike!' Helen quavered. 'How can I speak about this in a court of law? You w-wouldn't...'

'I would. In a small town like this, it'll make local headlines at the very least.'

Helen gasped, but managed to hold her tongue. She understood now what he was doing—the junior partner of a respectable firm of solicitors would certainly think twice before involving himself in any further scandal.

Philip Harkness had dropped his hand from his swollen jaw. 'That's blackmail.'

'You should know. Why don't you tidy yourself up, and take home your...' Mike ground to a pause, then started again '...your unlucky wife, before the bruising starts to show?'

The other man scrambled to his feet, and nervously straightened his tie. 'I'll get you for this, Armstrong.'

Mike laughed, a chilly, mirthless noise that made the hairs stand up on Helen's scalp. She bent swiftly to Betsy, burying her hands in the soft fur and straightening up only when she heard the door close.

'Now,' Mike grabbed her, 'let's have a look at you.'

'Let me go!'

She tried to struggle free, but it was no use. She couldn't escape the grip on her shoulders until he chose to let go, and pushed her roughly so that she in her turn flopped to the couch.

'I thought so,' he bit out in disgust. 'You've had too much to drink.'

'I have not!' She started to rise indignantly, and felt the room spin again. 'Have I?'

'Stay where you are.'

She sank back, unthinkingly obedient to the huge dark figure beyond the brightness of the desk-lamp. It moved to the door and disappeared, leaving her wondering why he'd left her there. She found out the answer when he reappeared with a tray, which he set on her lap before he sat by her and removed a plate for himself.

'Get that into you,' he snapped, 'and we'll see if it does any good.'

She rose at once to the curt tone. 'Any good for what? I'm not...' She stopped, nose quivering like Betsy's. 'Is that smoked salmon? And where on earth did they find asparagus this time of year?'

'Eat!'

'What are those?'

'Blinis.' He began on his own. 'Pancakes, with sour cream and caviare.'

She tried one, and it had gone almost before she'd tasted it. She hadn't realised how hungry she was, or how time had passed since her breakfast porridge and sandwich lunch.

'Look at these two,' she murmured fondly as the Labradors padded to her knees with melting glances. 'Slept through all the excitement, but the minute there's food about——'

'Spike, Duke,' he cut off her indulgent comment. *'Sit!'*

To Helen's amazement, both dogs scrambled back to their basket like naughty children. Betsy, who had been watching them disapprovingly from her own basket, looked smug.

'How did you manage that?' Helen asked, remembering how Charlotte Milburn spoiled her pets.

'Dogs are no different from people,' he told her curtly. 'They know who is and who isn't a soft touch.'

Chastened, she finished her food in silence. Once it had reached her, nothing seemed quite so bad. Nothing really mattered, after all, except maybe just snatching a nap on this lovely, solid head-rest she seemed to have found...

'Wake up!' His voice was sharp, and he was lifting her head from his shoulder. 'We're not there yet.'

'Hm?' She opened her eyes. 'Not where?'

He settled her head against the armrest. Which wasn't so good, but she'd make do with it. She closed her eyes again, and drifted into a swirling, singing darkness that went on and on.

On and on, until strong hands shook her out of it. A muscular arm propped her up, the unmistakable freshness of good black coffee drifted up to her, and she drank.

'I'd fetch some more,' frosty as ever, he put the empty cup on a table, 'but there's a limit to what it can do. You had three of those champagne things while I was watching.'

'Watching?' Helen's mind cleared as the coffee took hold. 'And why did you think you'd any business doing that?'

'Come on.' He stood up, brushing the question aside like a cobweb. 'Now I've neutralised some of the alcohol, I'm taking you home.'

'But I've got my car here...'

'You think you're in any state to drive?'

'But how will I get it back?'

'You can work on that one tomorrow. It might help with the hangover.' He pulled her to her feet. 'Can you walk?'

'Of course I can, and drive too...'

She stopped. The room was dancing again, though slower than before. Biting her lip, she admitted to herself that she really wasn't fit to drive, and concentrated on making her farewells and explaining about her car. And then she was out in the cold and the dark, with Betsy at her heels and Mike following.

Only when she sank into the luxurious upholstery of his car did she falter. 'I forgot Betsy's basket.'

'I didn't.'

Somehow, he'd already got it into the back. Cold air blew over her from the open rear door, and she pulled up the collar of her heavy coat. If she kept her mind on small things like this, the cold and her collar, maybe her heart would stop knocking against her ribs.

And still it knocked. She was surprised he couldn't hear it over the quiet purring of the car.

Or perhaps he could. Wordless, together yet apart, they glided out of the little town and zig-zagged through the country lanes. Only on the wide reaches of the moor did he throw a question, hard-edged as a weapon.

'Remember this place?'

'It's where we first met,' she answered timidly.

It looked peaceful enough now, the half-moon silvering the heather and the homeward road stretching over the next hill. But when she dared to glance at him, the tiny glow of the instrument panel might have been the lightning-flash all over again. Mouth long and sardonic, winged eyebrows flaring to the wide temples, he stared ahead like a hawk, a hunter, the devil out for prey.

She mustn't think of him like that. She must speak again, make him speak again, rout these evil images from her mind.

She tried for a light tone. 'You're very quiet.'

It didn't work. His mouth only went tighter, his eyes blacker and more shadowed. 'Do you wonder?'

She shivered at his anger. And still every note of that deep voice jumped in her blood, sang in her nerves so that she wanted to sing back, to answer some question he hadn't asked.

He changed gear for the last hill. 'How did you come to be in there with that...that tom-cat?'

'I don't know,' she answered, honestly bewildered. 'I mean, I was talking to Betsy, and there he was.'

'On that damned couch with you?'

'Not...not straight away. I—sort of—let him have the seat next to me.'

He made a wordless noise of disgust, and she rushed on.

'Only because I thought he was feeling a bit—er—well, a bit the way I was feeling.'

'You mean,' he threw the word brutally at her, 'drunk.'

'I was *not*!' Really, only a saint would take this kind of talk. 'I don't even *like* champagne.'

'Then you should damn well be more careful with it.' He brought them to a halt before the house and switched off the engine. 'Can you make it down those stairs on your own?'

'Oh, you...'

She tore her keys from her bag and scrambled out. Drunk, indeed! She picked her way across the drive with special care in her high-heeled party shoes, just to prove how wrong he was. If she'd ever been even a little out of control, she certainly wasn't now. She could get her key into the lock, couldn't she? The door opened, and Betsy streaked across the drive into the house while Mike joined Helen on the porch.

'See?' She stared up at his black outline against the moonlit bushes. 'Am I acting drunk?'

'You're forgetting. I sobered you up.'

Unable to deny it, she shook her head. 'There's no point in standing here arguing...'

'None at all.'

And then he pulled her into his arms, and she couldn't draw back. Couldn't leave the warm darkness under his coat, couldn't deny herself the silk of his lapel beneath her cheek, the big, warm chest where the strong heart raced beneath her hand.

'Did he make a grab for you?' he asked huskily.

'No. Yes,' she admitted, shamefaced.

'Did he hurt you?'

'No—no, not really. But he wasn't...' Her hand, with a will of its own, strayed to his neck and lifted the smooth hair at the nape. 'He wasn't you, Mike.'

He kissed her, and she knew that his kisses were the only kind she wanted.

'This is how it should be, ' she murmured against his lips, and tasted them again.

How did her own coat come to be open. Perhaps, leaving the party in such disarray, she'd never closed it. And how had he found the snap-studs on this dress? Snap, snap, snap, and her breasts were defenceless in their lacy wisp of bra.

'Like fruit,' he exulted, taking them in his hands.

'Please,' she begged, not knowing if she meant him to stop or continue. 'Please.'

'Not fruit.' Endlessly gentle, he slid the lace away. 'Flowers. Just opening.'

She stared down at the two firm mounds, pale against the deep-coloured wool. Even in this near-darkness she could see, as well as feel, how they had gathered to thrusting peaks which clamoured for his touch.

'Just opening,' he repeated, and touched them.

Played with them until she knew exactly what he meant. Something was indeed opening within her, like a flower new to the sun. Opening and releasing a stream of sweetness which carried her along on its hot, demanding flood.

And if she went with it, who knew where it might take her? She tried to move, tried to speak, looked up into the deep-set eyes, and found no mercy in them. His hands held her breasts captive for his mouth to take, tasting, stroking, demanding until she couldn't bear the pleasure, the pain, the fullness and the longing to be filled. Then he pulled her close, and she felt, through all the layers of fabric, his maleness asserting itself.

Was she ready at last for this great unity which must surely change her life? Her body had only one answer—already her hand was poised on the door, ready to invite him to her bed. But another part of her held back, worried, nagged away in her head that this wasn't right, that she'd be sorry.

'You're a virgin, aren't you?' he whispered.

'Yes.' She sighed it out, grateful for his understanding. 'How did you know?'

'Because you're still afraid,' he answered, as he had once answered before. 'Don't be, Helen. I'd never, ever hurt you.'

'I know it.'

And she did, as certainly as she knew the pleasure he, and only he, could give her. But somehow it wasn't enough. She needed more than pleasure to stem this hot flood which pulsed within her.

'I'll take care of everything. Always.'

'Always?' She tilted her head back. 'That's a long time.'

'Not long enough. Not nearly long enough for all I want to do with you, Helen.'

He set his hands either side of her waist. His grip was gentle, caressing, and yet he held her firm. Firm as if he already possessed her. She remembered their first kiss, here on this porch, and stiffened with sudden understanding. No wonder her wiser self warned her to hold back.

'You still want Thornton Pele, don't you?'

He ran his fingers through her hair, so that it fell round her shoulders. 'Do we have to talk about that now?'

'Yes.' She pulled her head away.

He retained one curl, and breathed its fragrance. 'Nutmeg!'

'It isn't!' Galvanised, she sprang back. 'Leave me alone!'

'Helen, it's you I want. The house is the least——'

'I wouldn't let you buy it.' Free of him at last, she clutched her coat together like her tattered, recovered pride. 'And now you're trying to get it another way.'

She heard his fierce breathing, an in-and-out hiss above the sigh of the night wind. Then it quietened, as if he was gaining control of it, and perhaps of himself, too.

'You're obsessed with this place, aren't you?'

'It's mine.' She couldn't see the oak door at her back, but she could feel it, and take strength from it. 'Whatever you do, it's going to stay mine.'

'Noted.' He gave her a small, ironic bow. 'It can fall apart any way you want it to.'

'It *isn't* falling apart,' she stormed, grabbing the chance to contradict this monstrous, slanted view. 'Any more than Cuddymoor's a piece of scrubland...'

'A what?' He stared at her through the dimness. 'You've been talking to George Milburn.'

'Yes,' she snapped, fearful of betraying the catch in her voice. 'And if I'd known his party was for your wretched conservatory——'

'So you don't like that either?'

'As a matter of fact, I do,' she conceded, reluctantly truthful. 'What I didn't like was...' She swallowed, hardly able to say it. 'Was hearing you'd got planning permission.'

'Architects get lots of those.' Once more, his voice was hard-edged. 'But I suppose you mean the one for Cuddymoor?'

'You know damn well I do,' she flared, hating the way he was reducing her deep concern to a mere incident in his working life.

'And that's why you drank too much?'

'I didn't... I don't...' She shook her head angrily, but the awkward truth would not be dodged. 'Yes. I suppose it is.'

'So, because I'm building on a plot of land that's never been much use——'

'It isn't scrubland.'

'I never said it was. I said nothing at all to you this evening,' he pointed out mercilessly, 'until I found you in a mess, and had to help you out of it.'

'And a fine way you did that...'

She trailed into shamed silence. He'd been angry, yes, but he'd still got rid of her unwanted suitor. And she really couldn't have driven herself home, either.

'And you got into that mess,' he sounded even more incredulous, 'because you'd heard I can now start building on Cuddymoor? You're further gone than I thought.'

'I didn't know——'

'You don't know anything, it seems to me, except that this village has to stay feudal.'

'Feudal!' she repeated in outrage. 'That's a horrible thing to say. I've always——'

'You've always been the lady of the manor,' the deep voice cut through her like a whip. 'And you won't stand for competition from a Johnny-come-lately like me.'

'No, no, no,' she spluttered, caught completely off guard. 'I've never been a snob——'

'And aren't you proud of not being one?' he taunted. 'You, a Thornton of Thornton Pele, treating a peasant Armstrong as if he were your equal.'

'But you *are* my equal——'

'Wrong again. I'm your superior, and don't you forget it.'

He turned away, leaving her gasping with speechless fury, and came back with Betsy's basket.

'Where do you want this?'

She pointed a quivering finger to the tiles at her feet. Just let him offer to carry it downstairs for her, just let him!

He didn't. Instead he dumped it, straightened himself, and reached an arm out to her. She clenched her fists, ready to defend herself, but he only ran one of her curls through his fingers.

'Whisky to the Indians,' he murmured to himself, and dropped it back to her shoulder. 'Water under the bridge.'

So that really was how he saw it. She realised he was putting her out of his mind, and stumbled backwards into the doorway on a numb tide of anger. What was she doing here at all, with a man who treated her as a mere incident? A man whose real life was in tearing up and spoiling?

'Don't talk about bridges, Mike Armstrong. You aren't a builder, you're a destroyer.'

'Whatever I am, Helen Thornton,' he replied equably, 'I'm here to stay.'

'Not here.' She pounced on the chance to say it. 'Not in Thornton Pele. You're never setting foot here again.'

She closed the heavy oak door in his face, and leant against it for what seemed a long time. Presently, she heard his engine start up and throb into the distance, out of her life.

So, the last word of all had been hers. It was victory of a sort, so why did she find it so unsatisfying? She trailed across the hall, down the stairs, into the kitchen and that infuriating scent of nutmeg.

'Weren't you listening, Bridget?' she demanded of the desolate, scented air. 'It's over. What little there was. He's not the only one who can put an episode behind him and forget it.'

She needed to say it often as the days and weeks drew on. Never had early December seemed so dreary. She took none of her usual pleasure in the cheerful bustle of approaching Christmas, and escaped from it whenever she could to the windy moor, or to the paths by the river, which were slippery with dead leaves, where she walked Betsy every lunchtime.

In mid-December she had to attend the Christmas draw, to present her cake as one of the prizes. Mike Armstrong arrived after her and sat, absurdly oversized for the church hall's plastic chairs, near her in the front row.

After her first dismayed glance she never looked at him, but her body refused to be so disciplined. It stirred and quivered and glowed until she was glad of her heavy tweeds to hide its silent uproar. When young Mark Burrell won her cake, she stumbled to the front and shook hands in a daze.

'And who won the other prizes?' Meg asked during her weekly call. 'I suppose there was the usual bottle of sherry?'

'That went to the Fenwicks, I think.'

'You think?'

'I didn't stay. I was feeling a bit tired that evening.'

'So you don't know who got Mike Armstrong's portable radio?'

'I didn't even know he'd given one. Trust him.'

'Don't you mean, how generous?'

'No, I don't. When are you coming home, Mother?'

Meg was silent for a moment. 'It's so near Nora's time.'

'But she could hang on till Christmas.'

'I so much want to be here for it, darling. And maybe she'll start earlier.'

And with that Helen had to be content. She put down the phone, made her usual hot drink, and carried Betsy's basket into the boot-cupboard-bedroom as she did every night.

Life had become a matter of dreary routine. Get up in the dark, eat the porridge she had left the night before to cook slowly on the stove, put on her boring office clothes, start the car with increasing difficulty as the weather chilled, drive down the hill, and so to work.

Passing Cuddymoor, she always concentrated hard on the road ahead. That way, she could avoid seeing what was happening to her beloved trees.

This morning, though, her eyes were drawn to it from a distance. It was the hard-hatted, green-booted figure, taller than the others on the site, which compelled her attention.

Sure enough, it turned into Mike Armstrong. A roll of plans under his arm, he was consulting earnestly with someone who might have been the site foreman. As her little car approached he turned, almost as if he might have been looking out for it, and loped to the road verge to wave.

'You've got a nerve,' she muttered, and drove on as if she hadn't seen him.

Her satisfaction vanished long before she opened the office. It was the quiet period for tourists, and the routine winter chores were nothing like enough to occupy her. She lost count of the times she caught herself wondering why Mike Armstrong wanted to talk to her.

And always from there, her weary mind trudged its usual circle. Whisky to the Indians, water under the bridge. Her nerves jumped and pulled yet again, and she could almost see him, in that fur-collared coat over the bright designer sweater.

She blinked. No, it wasn't her rebellious imagination this time. It really was him, in chestnut-coloured tweed, the green boots replaced by chestnut-coloured brogues.

She shot to her feet. 'I'm just closing for lunch.'

'Thanks for a fine Northumbrian welcome.' He lingered in the doorway, blocking out the light. 'I wouldn't need to be here at all if you'd had the...' To judge from his expression, he'd been about to say something very rude. 'If,' he went on instead, 'you'd stopped when I called you this morning.'

She looked pointedly at her watch.

'You'd better accept this.' He approached her desk. 'Then I needn't take up any more of your valuable time.'

The package he laid on her blotter was tinsel-wrapped. Even as she drew away from it, her blood surged. Surely, after all they'd said to each other, he couldn't be offering her a present?

'I don't...' She coughed, and regained control of her vocal chords. 'I don't want anything from you.'

'This isn't from me,' he told her, equally frigid.

She squinted down at the package. 'So what is it?'

'You'd know, if you'd stayed to the end of the draw.'

She stared at him in horror. 'I didn't win your wretched radio?'

'Gracefully put. I suppose it's something if you're not throwing it at me.'

'I wouldn't be so wasteful,' she replied with dignity.

'Do I report to the committee that you've accepted it?'

'I suppose you'd better.'

'Right. See you around.'

He made for the door. Long before he reached it, Helen was conscious of her own churlishness.

After all, she'd enjoy this radio. And maybe, if she tried hard enough, she needn't think of him when she used it.

'Er—Mr Armstrong,' she called after him.

He paused, with the December wind whistling by him.

'Er—just . . .' She forced it out. 'Thank you.'

'My privilege, Miss Thornton.'

The papers whisked about on her desk, then settled as he closed the door. Through its glass, she saw him stride towards the corner, on his way presumably to the Grey Street car park.

'So he didn't really want to talk to me.' She unwrapped the parcel with her usual care. 'Any more than I did to him.'

She couldn't resist trying the radio. The choice of wavelengths was excellent, the tone clear and full. When a Strauss waltz soared up from it she switched it off in mid-swoon, bundled it into a drawer, and went out with Betsy into the bracing wind.

During the afternoon, she opened the drawer at intervals for a glimpse of her new, unexpected treasure. How maddening that she had Mike Armstrong to thank for it, when it was going to be so lovely having it. But she wouldn't let it bother her—no, she wouldn't. She closed the radio away with quiet firmness, to show how serious she could be, and moved to the leaflet stand.

It was, after all, a thoughtful prize to contribute. Anyone who won it, pensioner or teenager, was bound to welcome it. And, to judge from its quality, he hadn't hesitated over the price. He really was generous, just as her mother had said.

'Wake up, dear.'

Helen jumped, and looked round from her mechanical tidying.

'Are you sure you're quite well?' old Mrs Pringle enquired. 'We thought you might have caught something, when you couldn't stay to be given that beautiful radio...'

'I'm fine,' Helen said hastily. 'Do you want a lift home?'

'I've just said so, dear. I've still my prescription to fetch, and a stotty from the baker's, and with Christmas there's so much more shopping than usual...'

'No problem. I'll be ready at five-thirty prompt.'

Helen was as good as her word. Throughout the drive home, she kept her mind on the road. Once they were through the blow-by-blow account of the Christmas draw, the old lady's stream of chat became no more than a steady, soothing flow.

'You'll have heard the latest about Cuddymoor?' she asked as the lights of Linrother appeared in the distance.

Helen winced, slowed down, and let a van overtake. 'If you don't mind, I'd rather not talk about that.'

'Of course, dear,' Mrs Pringle murmured placidly. 'I'd forgotten—you were against it, weren't you?'

'Still am.'

'Oh, well. How's your mother getting on in Edinburgh? Staying on to see the new baby?'

'It looks like it,' Helen admitted, depressed.

They drew to the kerb. Afterwards, Helen took a miserable satisfaction from the way she carried in Mrs Pringle's shopping, made her farewells, got back to the car, and drove off, all without a single glance at the gold-lit windows of Moor Cottage on the other side of the road.

'After all,' she told Betsy as she set her new radio on her bedside table, 'we've plenty of other things to think about. Tomorrow evening we'll go out with the torch, and cut holly.'

On the phone a few minutes later, she didn't bother to ask how her mother knew of her win. Meg always enjoyed the Linrother grapevine, and presumably was still in touch with it by letter and phone.

'When did he hand it over?' she asked.

'Lunchtime,' Helen snapped. 'And I thanked him, if that's what you're getting at.'

The line hummed with silence.

'I did,' she protested to the unspoken criticism.

But, after all, Meg had something else on her mind. 'I'm sorry, darling,' she said when she explained it. 'But having stayed this long——'

'You just enjoy the new baby when it comes.' Helen made her voice as cheerful as possible. 'And keep Nora's spirits up during the waiting.'

'You could travel here?'

'I'll think about it.'

'You won't,' Meg said with resignation.

'Don't worry, I'll be fine. There's always Betsy.'

'Ah, yes. Betsy, and the radio. It's nice to know somebody's looking after you.'

'Nobody needs to,' Helen said quickly. 'I can take care of myself. Let me know the minute anything happens, now.'

When she put down the phone, Betsy padded across and looked up into her eyes. Helen stroked her, then slid from her chair to the floor, hugged her close, and tried not to think about the dismal prospect of spending Christmas all alone at Thornton Pele.

CHAPTER SEVEN

DECEMBER continued fine but cold. The robin came back to its ledge under the porch roof, and the crumbs Helen scattered on the front lawn each morning attracted even the shyer birds.

Not that she saw them, except at the weekend. She had to take their plate to the garden in the early-morning darkness, then go in and eat her own breakfast by electric light. Only as she was driving to work was the daylight strong enough to see by.

And a lot of good that was. In spite of all her efforts, she couldn't help noticing that something new was happening at Cuddymoor. Further space had been cleared, and a great rectangular hole dug through the thistles and coarse grass.

'I see the swimming pool's coming on,' young Robby Burrell remarked when she gave him a lift home from the Tech. 'Mr Armstrong says he'll open it to the village, certain evenings.'

'Big of him.' Helen kept her eyes ahead.

'Did you know I'll be working there?' Robby ventured with teenage awkwardness. 'I start in the summer.'

'A holiday job?'

'No, it'll be permanent.'

'Why, that's marvellous!' Helen drew up at his parents' front gate. 'And so near home. Is your mother thrilled?'

'You bet.' His smile was much more relaxed as he opened the passenger door. 'She already sees me as head groundsman.'

'Will there be that many of you?'

'Three. We'll have fruit trees to look after, and vegetables for the kitchen.'

Clearly, these pampered guests were to have only the best home-grown produce. Helen kept the thought to herself. 'You'll have your work cut out, growing crops on that land.'

'You wait till we've gone over it. Mr Armstrong says——'

Helen shifted restlessly. 'Your mother seems to want you.'

Linda Burrell was at the window. Lit by the Christmas tree beside her, she signalled with some urgency.

'She thinks I'll forget.' Robby got out and waved. 'I've to tell you, the carols is at our house tonight.'

Helen glanced along the street under its archway of lights. 'I thought the Simons were having the meeting at their place?'

'They were, but their baby cries all the time. She's more of a handful,' Robby announced, complacently masculine, 'than any of the boys were.'

Helen put the engine in gear. 'Shall I call for you tomorrow?'

'Please. My bike's off the road till the end of the week.'

'See you, then. And tell your mother I'll be there.'

The weekend-before-Christmas carols were a long-standing custom with the Linrother women. This planning session beforehand was an important part of the ritual, and usually Helen looked forward to it. Even feeling as she did at the moment, she didn't want to miss it. One way and another, she hadn't been much in the village lately.

You never know, she thought, packing the mince pies which were to be her contribution. I might enjoy it.

That particular hope soon faded. Robby let her in, and ushered her to a room full of animated talk which stilled as she appeared. Only Anne Simon continued, one eye on Helen.

'That pool's going to be a real asset to the village.'

'They'll enjoy it, too.' Linda Burrell put in. 'I like to think of them... Oh.' She turned in the lengthening silence. 'Er—nice to see you, Helen.'

Helen wished the others looked as if they agreed. Nobody spoke as she settled Betsy and took the remaining chair.

'I gather,' Anne Simon said at last, a defiant edge to her voice, 'you've heard of Mike's new plans?'

'Er—yes.' Helen turned quickly back to her hostess. 'I'm so glad about Robby's job.'

'Are you?' Anne demanded, determinedly aggressive. How thin she'd grown, and how drawn with fatigue—the new baby must indeed be difficult. 'Are you really glad?'

'It's good news for the Burrells,' Helen answered soothingly, and accepted a glass of ginger wine. 'What cause are we singing for this year?'

'Same as last,' Linda said, relieved to change the subject.

Anne, however, wasn't letting it go so easily. 'The rest of us *like* the idea of our helping along our heritage.'

'D-doesn't everybody?' Helen faltered.

'Do *you*?'

Helen put down her glass. 'Whatever's got into you, Anne?'

'I might ask the same question.' Anne's eyes swept over the peaceful Betsy. 'You seem more concerned with animals than with people, these days.'

'Can't I like both?'

'Apparently not.'

Helen made an effort, and held her tongue. This old friend wasn't herself, but why was she so intent on picking a fight?

Worse, as Helen looked round the room, she could see very little sympathy for her own dilemma. The other women were embarrassed, perhaps didn't like the open attack on her—but they weren't on her side.

'It's...it's Cuddymoor,' Linda explained, shamefaced. She brightened with sudden hope. 'I suppose you might have changed your mind, now you've had time to think about it?'

'Of course I haven't!' Helen wondered if they'd all gone mad. 'Do we have to fall out over it? This is supposed to be the season of goodwill.'

'It's also the time,' Anne pointed out, 'when there was no room at the inn.'

'So what are you worried about?' Helen demanded, her Thornton blood fired at last. 'There's going to be plenty here, when that monstrosity's finished.'

Now why on earth should this bring on another dreadful silence? They all knew her views—she had canvassed every house last autumn. Yet now nobody would meet her eyes except Anne, who continued to stare with something very like triumph.

'Er——' gentle Linda grabbed her action sheet '—here's the list I've typed out.'

She put all her authority as hostess into the words, and the tension eased. In a flurry of relief pens were brought out, diaries riffled open, and business commenced very much as usual. They were to start with old Mrs Pringle, who went to bed early and liked the 'Coventry' to soothe her down. They would finish as always at the pub, with 'Joy to the World'.

'What about Moor Cottage?' someone asked.

'Mike's away then,' Anne announced. 'He's asked us to keep an eye on the place, and he's already started off our collection very nicely.'

So that was that. Helen had been wondering how she would get through the Christmas season without running into Mike Armstrong and having to pretend a friendliness that she didn't feel. Now her problem had been solved. She ought to be delighted. Why wasn't she delighted?

'You *will* be delighted,' she told herself on the way home, 'if it kills you.'

The next morning, she felt as if it had. A huge rawness had invaded her nose and throat, her eyes might have been lined with sandpaper, and trying to talk produced a hit-or-miss noise like a broken squeaker.

'It'll go off,' she squeaked to the faintly disapproving Betsy. 'I'm fine really.'

Betsy sniffed, and Helen set doggedly about her morning chores. She wasn't going to admit how de-

pressing she found the idea of being ill here, all
alone. Her porridge tasted like cotton wool, but she
forced it down and convinced herself that she felt
better for it. After a cup of coffee she even had
enough voice to answer the phone.

'Robby's poorly,' Linda Burrell told her. 'Sore
throat, and then a temperature. We think it must
be that two-day bug they have at the Tech.'

Helen croaked her sympathy. 'He'll be over it by
Christmas.'

'Sure—but listen, are you all right?'

'Of course . . . excuse me . . .' Goodness, how it
hurt to cough!

'You'd better get back to bed,' Linda said,
alarmed.

'It's going off,' Helen croaked firmly. 'Give
Robby my regards, and tell him to get well soon.'

'Oh, *he'll* get well all right——'

'Good. See you at the carols on Saturday.'

Helen reached the end of the sentence and hung
up before she had to cough again. A glass of water
soothed her throat, but clearing the table and
washing-up seemed to take all her energy. She finished doggedly, then made her way to the coat cupboard and struggled into her heavy old tweed.
Oddly enough, it didn't make her feel any warmer.

'What I need,' she told herself, 'is to get going.'

Only somehow, that wasn't so easy. She was
already halfway up the stairs when she remembered
her torch, and had to go back for it. And the second
climb had suddenly become so steep, she took ages
getting to the top. She didn't dare look at her watch.

The dismal chill of the great hall brought on
another fit of coughing. She leant against the wall,

waited till she could drag in a whole lungful of the freezing air, got herself somehow to the front door, and opened it.

Mike Armstrong, fur-collared and enormous in the grey of first dawn, was jumping urgently from a blue Range Rover. At the sight of her, he slowed as if in relief.

'I'm in time, then. I thought you'd gone when I didn't see your car.'

Helen shivered. 'I keep it in the carriage-house these cold months.'

Suddenly, the job of opening those heavy carriage-house doors seemed more than she could cope with. And this new, thumping ache in her head made it hard to follow what he said.

'Linda called me. She's worried you may have Robby's bug, and drive when you're not fit.'

'As if I ever would!'

The nerve of the man, blocking her way like this! Not budging. Looking her over as if he didn't believe her. And, to make it worse, positively radiating health himself from leather boots to thick, shining hair.

'She says it hits very suddenly. One minute a sore throat, the next—wham.' He thumped his hands together, fist in palm.

Helen winced, then glared. 'Well, I haven't got it.'

It came out thick and slurred. Worse, the hostile tone must have got through to Betsy. She had been sniffing along a corner of the porch, but now she came back to sit at Helen's feet and gaze upwards. 'All right, all right.' Helen looked into the great, reproachful eyes. 'I know I've done it again.' She braced herself. 'Er—I didn't mean to be rude. It was—er—good of you...'

She leant against the door-jamb in despair. Would she have to go through life thanking him for one kindness or another?

'Do you often talk to Betsy like that?' he asked, somewhere a long way off.

'Doesn't everybody?' Further irritated because nothing she said came out right, she added, 'Talk to their dogs, I mean.'

'Well, yes. But not as if the dog had just told them what to do, and they were doing it.'

'Alice did.'

He was actually inside the door now, and catching hold of her. It was enough to make anybody want to collapse, being caught hold of like that. It made him so easy to lean against. Why did he go about encouraging people to lean against him? Why didn't he just let a person stand on her own two feet?

'And you still——' he asked somewhere above her head '—swear you're all right?'

What was it she'd been trying to say? 'Alice did. That is, I don't know if she met any dogs in Wonderland...'

'So that's where we are?'

'But all the animals ordered her about. She got quite annoyed about it.'

'Anybody would.'

'The cat made her watch mouseholes.'

'Have you a thermometer indoors?'

She tried to draw herself up. 'Are you implying I have a temperature?'

She did manage to say it, she was quite sure of that. It was only after she'd finished speaking that the whole world, lank shrubs and solid porch, dark drive and lightening sky, streamed together and whirled round her head.

Luckily, it all had a centre. A warm centre, strong and comforting, surrounding her and holding her up. Now it had scooped her off her feet. That was wrong—you didn't get picked up from your own doorstep, not by a man you weren't speaking to.

'I'm perfectly...able...'

'Stop wriggling.'

She didn't want to obey him. It was just so much easier, resting her cheek against his shoulder and letting things happen. There went the familiar sound of the door closing. And those little scratchy noises were Betsy, following over the parquet of the unsteady, darkish great hall. And here was the stairway door, tilting a bit as he opened it. And what was he on about?

'...stairs are a bit narrow.'

Trust him to find fault.

'They've been wide enough for two hundred years,' she retorted to his fur collar.

'I bet nobody's gone down them horizontal.'

'Who are you calling horizontal?'

She was almost sure she said it. If she didn't, she meant to. But how could a person say anything, tipped over his shoulder like this? She could hardly breathe, let alone speak. Luckily it didn't go on long; at the foot of the stairs he sort of rearranged her, and, when she was comfortable, she had to close her eyes for a minute.

She opened them with a start. 'Where are we?'

'Boot cupboard. Get that duvet back over you.'

She wasn't wearing her coat any more, or her jacket. There they were over the chair, with her shoes on the floor beneath. And she was on her bed, all ready to sink into it . . .

She jerked up and put her feet to the floor. 'I can't sleep with all my clothes on.'

'I was afraid you'd say that.'

She felt her head droop forward, blackness threatening to close in. 'Will you go away now, please?'

Had she been rude again? She must have been— he'd gone, and Betsy was looking sorrowfully across from her basket.

'I couldn't undress in front of him, could I?' she pleaded.

Betsy seemed doubtful, and maybe she was right. It was so lonely, levering yourself upright and stepping out of your skirt in slow motion. And who'd have thought it would be so difficult to take a sweater off? All it did was cling round your head, blinding you and making you wish you'd never started . . .

'Hold still!'

So he hadn't gone after all. He was here to help, brushing her shoulders and then her arms as he freed her gently from the muffling wool.

'Th-thank you.'

Shivering, she sat on the bed and huddled herself together, realising that her breasts were now covered only by a scrap of elasticated lace. She huddled tighter.

'My pyjamas are on that shelf . . .'

'I'll get them,' he announced promptly.

Then he was sliding her familiar knitted-cotton pyjama top over her head and pulling it down to her waist.

'Can you manage to get your arms into the sleeves?'

'Of course.' But she couldn't. She couldn't even make a start on it.

'What's the matter?' he asked.

'It's my...bra.' She went on struggling under the enveloping cotton. 'I...can't get it...undone.'

He sighed. 'Turn round.'

She obeyed, and let him unhook the back fastening. Light as a whisper, his fingers followed the straps upwards and drew them down from her shoulders.

His hands were so warm, so gentle, so clever. She would have liked them to stay with her, but they seemed to be doing their best not to. Working from the back, and under cover of her pyjama top, he brushed only the outer slopes of her breasts, and eased them free as gingerly as if they'd been explosive.

'Got it!'

She craned round. Breathing a little oddly, he held the scrap of lace aloft in triumph. When he found her watching, he dropped it on the bed, pulled a handkerchief from his pocket, and wiped his brow.

'All right, get on with it.'

Imprisoned within the top, careful to keep it decently pulled down, she tried to find the sleeves.

And tried. And tried.

'Cheer up.' He mopped her tears with that same useful handkerchief. 'It's not that bad. Here, give me your hand.'

He had slipped his own through one of the wrist-bands. When she obediently put hers into it, her arm slid into the sleeve with no trouble at all. The other arm followed with equal ease, and made her cosy right up to the neck and down to the wrists.

'Now.' He raised her feet to the bed and pushed her gently back on the pillow. 'For the love of heaven, wrap up and relax!'

She struggled up on one elbow. 'These tights tickle.'

'For goodness' sake, have I to take those off you next?'

'Of course not,' she croaked with dignity. 'If you'll just turn your back for a minute.'

He moved to the window and stared out, hands in pockets.

With enormous effort, she rose to her feet and wrestled down her thick, textured tights. By the time she was forced to sit down and rest, they were no further than her knees.

He glanced over his shoulder, then whirled round. 'Do you want to catch your death?'

He grabbed the bunched-up roll she had made of the tights, and pulled. They came off easily, though he was looking away as if he couldn't bear the sight of her.

'I suppose,' he dropped them by her bra, 'I ought to think myself lucky you weren't wearing suspenders.'

She wanted to ask what he had against suspenders, but her teeth were chattering too much.

Intent only on clearing the way for her pyjama bottoms, she plucked at the top of her briefs.

He grabbed her hand away. 'Oh, no you don't!'

She looked at him in alarm.

'You'll leave those on,' he told her. 'Or I'll... I'll... here!' He seized the trousers, squashed up one leg, and pushed her foot through it.

'All right,' she muttered, allowing him to do the same with the other, 'keep your hair on.'

'It's not my hair I'm worried about.'

She frowned, trying to work out what he meant. Then she gave it up, revelling in the snug grip of the fleecy material as she carefully drew it to her knees. After a moment he pulled her to her feet quite roughly, and before she could collapse he had the trousers settled and covering her.

'Are you satisfied?' He still sounded exasperated.

Humiliated by her own weakness, she nodded.

'Now, now, don't take it to heart.'

Gentle once more, he let her sink to the bed. The mattress might be old and lumpy, but it welcomed her like a friend. So did her duvet when it dropped on top of her, apparently out of nowhere. She coughed, sighed, curled up, and cuddled it over her head as she always did.

He must have switched on her new radio. It was playing very softly, a Rossini overture. No, not a Rossini overture, somebody singing. No, not singing, talking. Now it was music again, breaking in waves like the sea. Helen pushed back the duvet, and had to shield her eyes from the window.

'How did it get to be so bright?'

'It's a glorious afternoon,' he told her. 'Betsy and I are just going out to make the most of it.'

'That's nice. Betsy getting her walk.' She blinked round the room. 'It's warm, isn't it?'

'I've borrowed the Burrells' heater.'

She sat up, galvanised. 'What's it costing?'

'Let me worry about that.'

'You know I can't——'

'I'm the one who needs it. I'm working here today.'

He gestured to the corner, where her pier-glass had been pushed aside. The shelf she used as a dressing-table now held an open briefcase, and a litter of papers.

'Working here,' she muttered in her crackly, hit-and-miss voice. 'Why are you doing that?'

'I just thought I would. How do you feel?'

'I'm fine.' She raised her head, which insisted on drooping forward, and forced her eyes open. 'Thirsty, though.'

'Have some of this.'

He sat on the bed beside her, holding her up. What a marvellous way to be held up, by this great tweed-clad creature, raising this cup to your lips, so you could drink whatever it was, hot and soothing and delicious, right to the last drop.

'There's plenty more.'

'Thanks, I'm fine...'

The music had changed to something with a lilt. You could see the children dancing to it, in a circle, holding hands. Then they flew up into the pinkness, the blueness, the blackness.

Or perhaps it wasn't so black after all. There was quite a lot of light really, over in the corner where Mike sat writing. It was coming from the standard lamp behind his armchair...

Armchair? Standard lamp?

Yet this was still her bedroom. Beautifully tidy, with her clothes all put away, a vase of freesias on the bedside table, and Betsy contentedly asleep in her basket.

He looked up. 'Hello, again. Could you eat something?'

She shook her head.

'Right.' He stood up. 'Another hot drink.'

It wasn't a question, more an announcement. And then he vanished. So she was dreaming all this, just as she'd suspected, but it was a nice dream. Here he was at her side again in that soft chestnut sweater, offering that cup.

'Can you hold it yourself yet?'

And she could. And the drink was the same, a freshness in her dry mouth, a blandness in her poor throat.

'More?' He held up an insulated jug.

She could have managed some more, but perhaps she ought to be cautious. You never knew, with dreams.

'Where did it come from?'

'It's Linda's idea. I bought the lemons and the barley in town, and she made it after she'd tidied up.'

'Lemons and barley.' Helen slid down, and pulled the duvet over her. 'You didn't add anything else?'

'Like what?'

'It makes me so sleepy.'

'So I doped it?' He sounded amused.

'I only asked.'

'Go back to sleep.'

'There was something else,' she murmured into the pillow. 'I can still taste it.'

'You mean the nutmeg?'

'Is that where it's coming from?' she managed to say before the darkness closed in.

The next time she woke, she had to put on her bedside light. And there he still was, in what she now recognised as her own rocking-chair. Wrapped in a blanket, he slept with his head against the cushion she had embroidered at school.

It was nice seeing him asleep. His black hair stuck up in points against the linen cushion, and his face was smooth and innocent as a boy's. The light must be waking him, though. Already his eyes were opening, the hard lines etching round his mouth. He sat up, alert and commanding as ever.

'Don't you dare leave that bed.'

She continued to put her feet into her slippers. 'Certain things,' she croaked delicately, 'you have to get up for.'

'Oh. Right.'

He stood, yawning and stretching. In the same movement he took her blue woollen dressing-gown from its hook behind the door, and held it open for her.

'I'll give you five minutes, then I'll come and get you.'

'You wouldn't.' She pulled the dressing-gown tight.

'I would. In your bathroom, you could have frozen by then.'

'It's a perfectly good bathroom.'

'Stop arguing, and get going.'

'I was just about to.'

Satisfied to have the last word, she did. Long before the end of his five minutes she was back, so exhausted that she kicked off her slippers and tumbled into bed in her dressing-gown. When she realised her mistake, she struggled out of it.

'Here.' He reached her in one long stride. 'I'll take it.'

He did, and she flopped in relief on the lumpy mattress. Sunk among her pillows, she watched with blurred guilt as he settled in the rocking-chair.

'You can't be very comfortable there.'

'I am.' He replaced the cushion under his head, and rearranged his blanket. 'Very comfortable.'

She meant to speak again, but the dark got in the way. Or did it? Wasn't it daylight glimmering round the wall outside her window? She put on her light, found the hands of her clock at eight, and blinked sadly at the corner where he'd been.

'Good morning.'

'Mike!' she exclaimed, smiling. 'I thought I'd dreamt you.'

'Some dream, that puts on your radio.' He switched it to soft, skippety morning music while he nodded at the rocking-chair. 'And moves your furniture about.'

'But the cushion and blanket were gone.'

'I tidied up. Are you ready for your breakfast?'

He'd made tea, and just the way she liked it. After that, the soft-boiled egg slipped down so easily, she was rather glad he wasn't in there to witness her greed. By the time he returned, she had finished off the last of the buttered toast with some of her mother's heather honey.

'I see you're back with us.' He piled the empty plates together approvingly.

She picked up the holly spray, two leaves and three berries, which he had put on the white tray-cloth. 'Was I awful?'

'Well. Your best friend wouldn't call you an easy patient.'

'My best friend,' she repeated bleakly. 'That used to be Anne Simon.'

'Anne has her worries. Now, are you going to be good?'

'As you've been to me, you mean?' She played with the prickly holly leaves, trying to sort out her jumbled, feverish memories. 'Spending the night in that chair——'

'Don't change the subject. Will you rest, and keep warm?'

'Will you feed the birds for me?'

'You drive a hard bargain.'

'And walk Betsy?'

'She's coming with me for the day.'

'Those are the important things, then.'

'Not all of them. But Linda's bringing soup for your lunch, and the casserole she's made for our supper.'

'That's good of her,' Helen observed humbly, 'with Robby to look after.'

'He's nearly better already. As you'll be, if you keep warm.'

'Warm.' She searched in her mind through the disconnected scenes which were all she had of the last twenty-four hours. 'Didn't you say *you* needed it warm in here to work?'

'Your temperature was a hundred and two. I'd have said anything to keep you quiet.' He smiled that crooked, devilish smile. 'But, in fact, I did get some work done.'

She stared at his briefcase, which was waiting by the door full of plans for the destruction of Cuddymoor. How ironic, how bitter, that her weakness had brought them right here into her home.

'I hear they're to have a swimming pool.'

'We've settled that.' He pulled out his gold hunter watch, checking it against the radio time-signal. 'I'll tell you more about it this evening, if you like.'

'What makes you think I'd want to know?'

'You still don't?' He looked taken aback.

'Why should I?'

She wanted to hate him, but her conscience wouldn't let her. Heaven knew what she'd have done without him. And he must have cancelled plans, broken appointments, made a complete mess of his working day, to take care of her like this. You didn't have to agree with what he was doing, to appreciate his generosity.

Yet here she was, hardly able to look at him for resentment. It was a positive relief when he shrugged, and left the room.

He returned almost at once with the insulated jug and a cup. He set them on the tray beside her, and eyed her coolly. 'Here's the doped lemon barley water. Seeing I'm taking the bugged dog away.'

'I didn't really think——'

'Is there,' he cut her short, glancing round the room, 'anything else you might want?'

'I really didn't——'

'Save it. I'm running late.'

She stared at the window, and the wall beyond it. So he really was going away. Well, for all she cared, he needn't ever come back. But even as she thought of it her heart lurched with the sense of loss.

'Is it all right if I take these,' he waved her keys, 'to let myself in this evening when I bring Betsy home?'

She nodded, feeling suddenly tremendous. Like a watered flower. Strong enough to run a marathon. She smiled at the thought of flowers running marathons, and curled up again. Only, wasn't there something? Something important? 'Er—Mike?'

Her voice was still weak, but he'd heard. He was at the door, waiting.

'It's just . . .' She swallowed. Knowing how much time she had already cost him made it even harder to get out. Yet she must say it.

'Just, thank you.'

And then his smile wasn't at all devilish. Not devilish at all, only sympathetic and tender as he left the door and moved swiftly to the bed. Now he was bending over her, his face near hers, his lips gentle on her cheek for the briefest of moments before he stood up once more.

'It was my pleasure. Can you sleep again, do you think?'

She sighed, and settled the duvet round her. 'Now I can.'

CHAPTER EIGHT

'WHAT the——?' Mike leapt into the room, and banged the door shut on the freezing draught. 'What are you doing?'

Helen whipped the towel around herself sarong-style, and tried to answer. The effort made her cough, so she reached crossly for the radio, switched off the brass-band Christmas carols, and tried again. 'Drying myself. What does it look like?'

His gaze rose from her long, bare legs to her shining wet shoulders. 'Catching pneumonia is what it looks like.'

'It was warm as anything,' she flung an indignant arm at the heater, and at the low red sunlight, ''till you let in the cold.'

'I shut the door as quick as I could.'

'Haven't you heard of knocking?'

'Would it have done any good?'

She did see what he meant. Perhaps the radio had been rather loud. With all the splashing and rinsing, she certainly hadn't heard him arrive at the house, and she might equally have missed a knock on her door.

'You could at least have tried,' she countered. 'Anyway, what are you doing here so early in the afternoon?'

He wasn't listening. 'Is that the biggest towel you have?'

She looked down, and grabbed it together. Even then it didn't cover enough of the bits she wanted covered, and her embarrassed, heaving breasts were more than half on view. And it wasn't as if she looked glamorous. She resisted the impulse to tear off her blue bath-cap, anchored the towel firmly under her arms, and drew a cautious breath.

'This is my room, Mike. I'm entitled to be private in it.'

At last she'd got through to him. He blinked, and dragged his glance away from her.

'Quite right.' He smiled that crooked, disarming, completely human smile she had once thought so devilish. 'Looking after you must bring out the bully in me.'

'It certainly does.'

But, even while she spoke, she had to remember how much she owed him. He'd stayed here when she'd needed him, coming and going at her bedside, caring for her when she couldn't so much as think straight. And now she was complaining because he hadn't knocked.

'Seeing you're better, I'll have to change my ways.'

Eyes away from her, he dumped the suitcase he was carrying on a handy shelf, and opened it. Still not looking at her, he took out a dark brown robe and shook it to its full length.

'Turn round.'

'Some change.' She clutched her towel tighter. 'You're still giving orders.'

'Just turn. Then you can argue all you like.'

'I don't want to argue, I want to finish drying myself——' She broke off when she realised that, for all her protests, she'd turned just as he'd ordered. A warm, enveloping cloud of towelling settled around her.

She let her own damp towel drop to her feet, and felt her heart begin to race. He was so close. The back of her neck crackled with his closeness, and a pulse in her throat hammered as his capable hands flicked the edges of the robe together under her chin.

'Why on earth . . . ?' She licked her lips, and tried again. 'Why have you brought this here?'

'I just . . .' He, too, seemed to be having trouble talking. 'Just thought I would.'

His hand was still across her shoulder, holding the robe. Slowly, unable to stop herself, she leant back and rested on that great, strong wall of a chest, rubbing her head against it. Her bath-cap rustled away—who knew where?—and her hair uncoiled.

She heard his breath hiss through his teeth. Then his face was buried in her hair, and his hand had found her breasts under the robe. While his lips travelled from her temple to her cheek to the sensitive curve of her jaw, his stroking fingertips danced on her breasts until she couldn't stay still, had to respond, had to turn, fling her arms round his neck, meet the fierce claims of his mouth with her own.

His body, too, was making its claims. But no—as her hands pressed against the heavy wool of his sweater, and she savoured the play of muscle beneath, she knew that this was no claim but an offering. And at last, at last, she was ready to accept what he offered.

'Let me look at you.' He held her away and opened the robe wide.

Greatly daring, Helen shook herself free of it, and held out her arms to him.

Still he devoured her with his eyes. 'Have you the least idea how beautiful you are?'

Unable to speak, she surged back to his embrace. Nobody else had seen her like this, and nobody else ever would, she thought as his mouth traced a hot, tantalising track from her neck to her shoulder to her breasts.

'Ivory,' he murmured against her flesh. 'No, silk. Ivory silk, and pink pearls.'

He took both pearls at once, lips closing on one while his fingers surrounded and teased the other. Then that, too, surrendered to his mouth, and his hands smoothed their way down her body, and she cried aloud with pleasure.

And the cry changed to a cough, and the cough wouldn't stop.

When he lifted her to the bed, she was still coughing. When he covered her with the duvet and disappeared, all she could do was go on coughing. When he returned with the lemon barley water, she drank it eagerly. Gradually her cough stilled, and she sank back exhausted on the pillow.

He indicated her discarded pyjamas, flung over his shoulder. 'Shall I put these in the linen-box?'

She nodded, not daring to speak, and brought an arm from the duvet to indicate the china bowl she had used for washing. Rather than freeze in the bathroom, she had fetched water from the kitchen, but she couldn't see herself finding the strength to carry it out.

'Stay quiet, now. And—er——' he glanced at the clean pyjamas she had put at the foot of the bed. 'Can you—er—get into those without help?'

'Of course I can,' she burst out indignantly. 'Whatever makes you——?' Another fit of coughing interrupted her.

'Don't try to talk.' Suddenly gentle, he poured more lemon barley water. 'You,' he went on to her enforced silence, 'have been what my family call making too free. And so, heaven help me,' he brought the clean pyjamas to her, 'have I. Now, put these on, and I'll send in Betsy.'

Betsy! Helen shot upright against her pillows.

He answered her unspoken question. 'I had to close the door fast, remember?'

As if that were any excuse for leaving the poor darling out there on her own all this time! She was almost indignant enough to try and tell him so, when he leant forward and pulled the duvet up over her breasts.

'Don't do that, my sweet. It's bad for my blood-pressure.'

He might talk about blood-pressure, but when he lifted her washing-bowl the water in it barely trembled. She watched him depart with it, waiting for her own foolish agitation to fade. It did, leaving nothing but weariness, and she had to summon all her strength to rise and put on her clean pyjamas.

These were of the same clinging knitted cotton as those she had just discarded. She pulled the dark blue top over her head and frowned, trying to capture an elusive memory. Hadn't she, at some time during her illness, had trouble with something like this? And hadn't he helped her?

She let it go, and dragged a comb through her hair. At least the coughing fit seemed well over, so she could use her voice again when Betsy decorously greeted her.

'Hello, darling.' She stroked the floppy ears. 'Lovely to see you back. Which reminds me,' she added as Mike followed. 'You haven't told me why you left work so early.'

He closed the door. 'Why aren't you in bed?'

She showed him the floor-length blue wool dressing-gown she had taken from its hook. 'I'm going to sit in the kitchen.'

'Now, Helen——'

'Honestly, I'm much better. And it's warm in there.'

'It's warm here.' He stayed solid between her and the door.

'Is this how you change your ways?'

'Is this how you try to be a good patient?'

'Dammit, Mike!' All the angrier for her aching bones and heavy eyelids, she sank to the bed. 'You could keep me a prisoner here the rest of my life.'

'Only till suppertime.' He took the dressing-gown. 'If you rest now, that is.'

'Oh, all right.' Though she agreed so unwillingly, she was glad to stretch out again. 'Why did you bring that suitcase? Are you staying the night?'

He closed it to take away. 'I talked to your mother. We reckoned one more night would see you through.'

'So you'll use her room?'

'That's what I agreed with her. I've brought sheets.'

'Didn't you think ours would be good enough?'

As soon as it was out, she hated herself. However tired, however ill, she'd no excuse for such rudeness. It would have been bad enough any time, but just now it was unforgivable.

'I wanted,' he explained with a hint of impatience, 'to save you trouble.'

'I'm . . . sorry.'

He approached, stared at her with a small frown. 'Let's hope you haven't overdone things.'

'If I did,' she heard the sharpness in her own voice, but couldn't stem it, 'you helped me.'

'Guilty as charged,' he admitted, his own impatience more marked. 'On the other hand, if I'd been here, I'd never have let you out of bed at all.'

'This is my house, and I'll do what I like in it.' Even as she spoke she squirmed at the childishness, and slid down to hide under the duvet.

'If you aren't the most infuriating little——' He made a bitten-off pause. 'Listen, grouch. We're both tired, we're both hungry, and we're both . . . disappointed.'

'I'm *not* disappointed!' she denied hotly, raising herself on one elbow the better to convince him. 'How could I be, when I don't . . . when I've never . . . ?' She gave up, and flung herself over to face the wall. 'You said I had to rest.'

He must have gone very quietly. She didn't hear him leave, only the door softly closing. She opened her eyes, and the glory of the winter sunset was a mere dazzle in the empty room. She might just as well rest her poor, tired eyes, she thought, shutting them and putting an arm down for Betsy.

No cold nose sniffed at her questing hand, so Betsy had gone, too.

'She deserves a better owner, anyway.' Helen humped the duvet round herself. 'I'm not fit to have such a nice dog. Or such a nice man...'

Nice? When he'd just nearly seduced her? When he'd wanted her home from over her head? When he was putting up a building which would change the character of the village forever?

She pushed at the pillow. 'If it hadn't been for that fit of coughing...'

But her mind shied away from the memory of his caresses. She stared at the ceiling, and forced herself instead to be realistic. Yes, he'd roused her in a way she wouldn't have thought possible. But what did that mean, except that he was a skilful lover?

'As good at getting his own way with women as he is with land,' she thought bitterly. 'With everything, in fact.'

That was it—everything had to be his way. Wherever he was, whatever he did, Mike Armstrong had to be boss.

'He's already boss of Cuddymoor,' she reminded herself with sleepy resolution. 'And got the whole village on his side. But he isn't ever going to boss me. Not me.'

The damp-stains on the ceiling became a neat, white-capped figure. 'You and your scent of nutmeg.' Helen turned on her side, not to see Bridget in her grey and white uniform.

When had the sky outside the window darkened? And why was Bridget rapping that nutmeg against her wooden spoon? Rapping and rapping...

Helen sat up, and put on the bedside light. 'Come in.'

Mike had taken off his jacket and sweater. Over his green shirt and darker green trousers he wore a practical apron of brilliant yellow cotton.

Relaxed after her sleep, she couldn't help smiling. 'You look like a buttercup.'

'Buttercup yourself.' He came over and smoothed her hair from her brow. 'Or maybe marigold's more like it, with you.'

She sat up hastily. 'What's that toasty smell?'

'Supper's ready.'

'I don't know if I want any food.' But the words reminded her how ungracious she'd already been. 'It's hard to work up an appetite,' she added hastily, 'when you're doing nothing.'

'You haven't done as much nothing as you should have.' He studied her. 'The cough's better?'

She nodded. 'I think I must have slept.'

'It's thirsty work, sleeping. You'd better have a sherry.'

'There isn't any——' She stopped, caught in mid-breath by a sudden, vivid picture of a schooner of Amontillado, tawny with the light behind it. 'You've brought some?'

'It's waiting.'

It was, on the lacquer tray. The scrubbed kitchen table had been set with embroidered linen place-mats, and a silver vase of Christmas roses, and red candles in a silver stand.

He struck a match with satisfaction. 'Linda certainly knows how a table should look.'

'She gave me a super lunch.' Helen stroked Betsy, who had come up to say hello in the serene radiance of the little flames. 'But all this—what a lot of trouble she's gone to!'

'She's on cloud nine at the moment, over Robby's job.'

'Of course,' Helen answered flatly. 'At Cuddymoor.'

'Now don't start.' He drew back her chair. 'Come on, let's get you settled.'

And settled she was. In the warmest place at the table, with a brilliant wool rug round her knees, and the subtle, autumn flavours of the sherry on her palate. Oh, dear, no wonder it was so hard to hate him, she thought. He raised his glass to her, then forgot to drink from it because he needed a serving spoon, and had to find one in the table drawer.

'*My* table drawer. *My* serving spoon,' she reminded herself, and saw the answer in her mind as if in a parallel list. *His* time, *his* trouble, *his* caring. All unaware of the argument she was having with herself, he brought over the casserole.

'Lucky I gave Linda so many of these for her freezer.' He served her a small, perfect trout. 'Shall I fillet yours?'

'There you go again! What kind of a fool do you——?' She broke off, ashamed. 'Thank you,' she went on with more dignity. 'I can do it.'

And she did, very neatly, before eating every scrap. The toasty things turned out to be almonds, scattered over a white wine sauce with mushrooms, and set off by tiny new potatoes. And, when that was finished, he fetched from the pantry two feather-light baked custards.

'With nutmeg!' she exclaimed. 'Did Linda make these, too?'

He shook his head. 'They're from that delicatessen on Grey Street. You have to order them specially.'

'That shop's fearfully expensive,' she commented, economy-minded from old habit, and added quickly, 'Of course, it's different for you.'

'Is it?' he asked, suddenly curt.

'I m-mean,' she stammered, trying to cover her blunder, 'they're delicious, and I'm glad you bought them . . .'

'So that's all right, then.'

Hearing the dry tone, she couldn't meet his eye. Instead, she looked down at her custard, which suddenly didn't taste of anything.

'Come on, eat up,' he mocked her. 'You might as well enjoy it, after I've paid all that money for it.'

'I d-didn't m-mean——'

'Yes, you did.' He finished his own doggedly, without appetite. 'Same as you always do.'

'I'm sorry, Mike. It was a stupid thing to say.'

'If you mean just now, that's the least of it.' He put down his spoon, and leant back in his chair. 'What I'm talking about has been going on ever since we first met.'

She stared mournfully down at her place-mat. She didn't need to ask what he meant.

'The same thing, over and over again,' he growled, pushing away his empty dessert goblet on its silver saucer. 'And when you don't speak it, I always know you're thinking it.'

'About your having money.' She raised her head, and gathered courage to face him.

'I offer a decent sum for your house, and you act as if I were trying to steal it.'

'I didn't——'

'Then when I stumped up a radio for the Christmas draw——'

'I'm sorry!'

To her dismay, her eyes had filled with tears. She tried to shake them away, but they only broke free. While they ran down her cheeks, she pretended nothing was wrong and comforted the worried Betsy.

'There, now.' He dropped to her side straight-backed, an arm round her chair. 'It's nothing to cry about.'

'I'm n-not c-crying,' she sniffled.

'Of course you aren't.' He mopped her cheeks with the corner of his apron. 'I shouldn't have gone for you like that.'

'You d-didn't . . . you n-needn't think . . .' She gulped, trying to make sense. 'I c-can g-give as g-good as I g-get.'

'Don't I know it, you little border terror. Come on.' He rose with an air of determination. 'Let's put you back to bed.'

'No!' She sat bolt upright, refusing to think what might happen if he came to her room while she felt so soft and melting and in the wrong. 'C-can't we sit a while first? Just s-sit,' she added carefully, 'and talk.'

'If you'll stop crying.'

'There.' She wrestled back a sob. 'I've stopped. If I ever had been, that is.'

He grinned, and offered his arm. 'Come on. Your rocking-chair's waiting.'

She rose, and draped the beautiful rug majestically about her. 'Do I look as if I need help to walk?'

Alas, the rug was caught under the leg of her chair, and she staggered at the first step. And, when he steadied her, she found it easier after all just to take his offered arm.

What a long way to the sitting-corner, and how strong his arm under her hand. How marvellous it would be to have an arm like this, yours against the world, for ever and ever.

And why would she want a thing like that? To distract herself from such thoughts, she paid attention to the tune which was running through her head, and tried it over in a cracked hum.

'"...old rockin'-chair will get me."' She sank thankfully into it. 'Where does that come from?'

'"Stormy Weather".' He wrapped her in the rug. 'Your song. Now stay there, and be good.'

While the reassured Betsy settled alongside in her basket, he crossed to the dresser. When he returned, he held two brandy balloons, a spoonful of golden liquid in each.

'This should complete the cure.'

'Won't it just!' She accepted her glass and wet her lips at the potent, fire-scented contents. 'You can't think how much better I feel.'

'I can see you're stronger.' He turned out the light over the table, and dropped his apron to a chair. 'You're sure you won't try this custard again?'

'You know, I believe I could.'

And she did, chasing every last morsel in the little cup with careful, endless probings of the silver spoon.

'Why don't you lick it?' he suggested, amused.

'No, I've got all I can...oh. You're teasing.'

'Little ginger cat.' He lowered himself to the other rocker. 'Did you say you wanted to talk?'

'Well...' She paused, wondering where to begin. Unspoken, unspeakable thoughts raced through her mind.

I know we nearly made love just now, she might have said. But it meant nothing unless you...

Unless you love me. Her lips silently formed the words, and she glanced at him in dismay. It was all right, his eyes were closed. He hadn't seen, and would never, ever hear her say it. She wouldn't even think it.

How could she ever have thought of him as a devil? Look at him now, mouth vulnerable, big hands resting on the arms of the rocker as if still ready to help wherever help was needed. Well-kept hands, they were, but roughened along the index fingers. Probably the downturned, invisible palms were roughened more—these hands would never mind getting dirty.

She sipped her brandy. 'Mike.'

'Yes, sweetheart?'

Her blood leapt. Supposing he meant it? But no, it was only a word. He probably didn't even know he was saying it. He was probably half-asleep, behind those closed eyelids.

'You've done an awful lot for me, haven't you?' she began, very low so as not to disturb the rest he had so richly earned.

'Careful.' He dragged his eyes open. 'If you start crying again, your feet won't touch the ground.'

She managed a weak giggle. 'You mean, you'll carry me?'

'Why not? I already have.'

So he had, a few hours ago, when they'd nearly... She hastily looked away from him. If she didn't think at once of something else, she would begin to remember his hands on her body. She raised the brandy bowl to her nose, but he must have noticed her blushes just the same.

'I didn't mean then,' he told her, rather fast, 'I meant yesterday morning. I brought you all the way down from your front door.'

'Did you?' Jumbled, appalling memories whirled before her, and she was distracted—as he'd meant her to be. 'I must have been a right nuisance to you, one way and another.'

'Mm.' He closed his eyes again. 'I've certainly always known you were around.'

'Is it any good if I promise——'

'Not at all.' He stopped her with upraised hand. 'I don't believe in reformed characters. Though,' he opened his eyes, and met hers with a grin, 'I love it when you're this way.'

There it was again, the word love. Only, used like that, it didn't mean a thing.

'I might have been this way more often,' she answered with difficult humility, 'if it hadn't been for Cuddymoor.'

'And you,' he was suddenly observing her, heavy-eyed but alert, 'feel as strongly as ever about that?'

'I still don't want it, if that's what you mean.'

'I see.' His voice hardened. 'You're just against it, whatever the benefits?'

'What benefits? Are we to lose our privacy for a few jobs and the use of a swimming pool?'

'I wasn't meaning either of those things.' He slumped, as if weariness had really taken him over. 'But I suppose I should have known. Nothing's ever going to shift you, is it?'

Looking at the shadowed eyes, she had a sudden longing to comfort him. Yet how could she, if it meant pretending an enthusiasm she could never feel?

'I'm the only one in the whole village who hasn't come round to the idea,' she admitted. 'To hear the rest of them talk——'

'What are they saying?' he demanded, stiffening.

She shrugged. 'Only what's public knowledge.'

'The public knows nothing, and shouldn't be speaking as if it did.'

'Why shouldn't it?' she asked, confused. 'The plans are at County Hall for anybody to see.'

'Oh, that bit's sorted out. I still have to tell the old man, though.'

'Your father? But surely, if you need his permission——'

'Permission?' he echoed with a tired laugh. 'I've been a partner in the firm for years. It's his blessing I want.' He patted the place where his watch would be if he'd been wearing his waistcoat, and blinked at the old wall-clock. 'We ought to turn in. I want an early start in the morning, to get ahead of the Christmas traffic.'

'But that won't be too bad yet, will it?'

'It's building up. Thank heaven you're well enough to manage.' He eyed her with a curious new hardness. 'Linda's put a cold chicken in the fridge, and a quiche you can bake when you fancy something hot.' He brushed aside her thanks. 'You don't go carol-singing tomorrow, of course.'

'Tomorrow?' She frowned. 'Is it that soon?'

'Funny how the time passes when you're unconscious.' He closed his eyes again. 'Christmas is in three days.'

She kept her voice carefully level. 'And you're spending it with your family?'

He nodded, eyes still closed. 'Down in Berkshire.'

She felt suddenly empty. Not just unhappy but drained of feeling, wrung out and left on the grey shore of a grey sea. And you might as well get used to it, she told herself. This is how Christmas is going to be. You alone, he with the people who mean something to him.

They'd have presents, a tree, a meal. They'd be together as a family, and clearly that meant a lot to him. Look how he'd talked of wanting his father's blessing.

Which brought her back with a jolt to the thing she must say. Absolutely must. After she'd said it they could part, go to their separate beds and their separate lives, but here and now she must take her chance, and put the record straight.

'Mike,' she began softly. 'Are you listening?'

'Mm.'

'About Cuddymoor.'

'Mm.' He hadn't opened his eyes, but that was all right. That made it easier.

'I just wanted to say...maybe it isn't so bad.' There, it was out, and the rest could follow. 'Maybe it'll be all right, seeing *you're* building it. I...' She hesitated, then finished bravely. 'I trust you, Mike.'

No answer. He didn't want her olive branch.

Wait a minute, though. She leant round to look at him, and realised that wanting just didn't come into it. He was asleep.

'Right!' She stood up, full of good resolutions.

She'd wept all over him, snapped at him, wasted his time here because she'd wanted his company, and completely forgotten how tired he must be. Hadn't he spent the night on this same rocker, getting what sleep he could while he watched over her?

'This is why he came home early,' she observed to Betsy, 'because he was so tired.'

Betsy sighed, and closed her eyes.

'This time,' Helen raised her glass to each of them, and tossed off her brandy, 'it's my turn to help.'

But when she reached her mother's room, she found nothing left to do. The suitcase was open on the floor, a zipped leather toilet-kit on the dressing-table,. and the bed made up with brown sheets and pillowcases.

'Now what are you up to?'

She whirled round, and saw him leaning on the door-jamb. He advanced into the room. 'It's far too cold for you in here.'

'I wanted to make you comfortable,' she told him through chattering teeth. 'It seemed the least I could do.'

'Back to your own room at once!'

'You're ordering me about again.'

'I'll do more than that.' He reached her in one stride. 'I'll——'

He stopped. She stared up into the dark brown eyes, and then the only thing left to do was offer her lips.

This time there was no hesitation, no slow beginning. Desire rose hard and hot between them, washed fluid and hot around them, rushed them to a world where nothing mattered but mouth on mouth, lips tasting lips, tongue curling to tongue.

Then, in spite of her clinging resistance, he put her away from him. Gasping, aching, longing to be completely united with him, she watched him struggle for mastery of himself. Eyes full of banked-down yearning, he surveyed her high neckline.

'At least you're fully clothed.'

'Mike, I . . . Couldn't you . . . ?'

She floundered into defeated silence. How did you ask a man to take your clothes off, when he clearly had no intention of doing it? And besides, he was right—it *was* cold in here.

'Thanks to you,' she began, greatly daring, 'it's—er—warm in my room.'

He gulped, then turned her to the door and gave her a little push. 'So off you go to it.'

'You're . . . you're not going to help me?'

'Seeing it's just next door, I'm sure you can manage,' he told her huskily. 'I'll carry in Betsy's basket.'

'You needn't bother,' she rasped as her frustration turned to rage. 'I can perfectly——' But she had to break off as the cold at last took its toll, and a new fit of coughing shook her.

'Oh, for goodness' sake!'

Sounding at least as angry as she was, he put his hands either side of her waist and swung her off her feet. She stopped coughing from sheer surprise, but didn't have time to argue, let alone struggle. Before she knew what was happening, she was in the next room and dumped on her own bed.

'Now.' He whipped the cover over her. 'Will you stay there, and keep warm, and give a man some peace?'

'If peace is what you want,' she turned away from him on the pillow, 'it's all yours.'

'Don't you believe it,' he burst out as if goaded beyond endurance. 'I've had no peace since the first day I met you.'

She turned to face him. 'Then why——?'

'Is this how you want it to be, your first time? Between fits of coughing?'

She plucked at a printed rose on the duvet cover, not daring to meet his eyes. 'I won't always be coughing.'

'No, and you won't always be driving me mad, either. I'll get over you some day, Helen Thornton.'

'You'll what?' This time she had to look.

'Probably it'll be when you marry——' the dark eyes burned cold, merciless, devilish '——into another run-down county family like your own.'

'How . . . how dare you?'

'To a man like yourself, who wants everything exactly as it's always been,' he threw at her. 'You'd better save that virginity for him.'

She sat up in outrage, and was at once overtaken by the next fit of coughing. He grabbed the lemon barley water, and dashed some into the glass as if he hated it. She drank quickly, and thrust it back.

'It wouldn't have worked, Helen.' He set the glass on the bedside table with bitter care. 'I knew it already, but it's taken what you said this evening to convince me.'

'But what did I——?'

'Let's not go on about it.' He moved to the door. 'If I don't get some sleep, I'll be a menace on the road tomorrow.'

'But if only you'd——'

'Goodnight, Helen. Goodnight, and goodbye.'

CHAPTER NINE

'It occurred to me that you might think I'd taken her away for keeps,' Mike shouted over what sounded like a lorry passing. 'So I'm ringing to set your mind at rest.'

'Good of you,' Helen snapped. 'Though I'd rather you hadn't taken Betsy to Will Purvis at all.'

'I hope you're not thinking you'd have walked her yourself?' The lorry roar had faded, but another was beginning. 'I didn't waste my time looking after you just so you could put yourself straight back on the sick-list.'

'And I'm not about to take orders by long-distance phone, from——' The pips went, but she finished anyway. 'From a man who didn't have the courtesy to say goodbye before he left.'

'I left at six, and I'd said the only goodbyes that needed saying.' He fed in more coins. 'This is the last of my change, so listen, and listen good.'

'To you? Some hope.'

'You're staying indoors. Is that clear?'

'I'll make up my own mind about that.'

'*You are staying indoors!*'

Helen jumped, amazed at the volume he could force at her through the earpiece. The jump reminded her how shaky she still felt, but she couldn't give in to this kind of talk.

'Thank you for the call,' she said, with trembling but freezing courtesy. 'It was good of you to break your journey so that you could tell me what you'd done with my dog.'

'*Your* dog——' it sounded through gritted teeth '—needs her exercise like any other. And *you* aren't fit to give it.'

'Excuse me, but my breakfast's getting cold.'

She heard the loud click at the other end of the line with some satisfaction. She'd had the last word again.

Not that it made her cooling porridge any more appetising. She swallowed it down, and brooded once more about the way he'd suddenly begun insulting her last night. What had she said to provoke such an onslaught? Her mind recoiled from his words, but they haunted her, just as they had through the night. So she was destined to marry a man from a run-down county family like her own, was she? And she'd better save her...

But no, she couldn't think about that. If she thought about that, she'd put her head on the table and cry. How could he say those things? How could he even think them, when he must know that she couldn't bear the idea of making love with any man but him?

She'd been quite sure she hadn't slept at all. But she must have, because in the morning she'd found Betsy gone from her room. So he'd taken her pet, and gone away, and left her alone in this empty, echoing, dismal...

'That's enough!' she admonished herself. 'It's Thornton Pele we're talking about. Your home.'

Which didn't make it any more cheerful, but she'd do something about that. She couldn't go out and cut holly—she knew quite well, as she crossly declared in yet another imaginary argument with

Mike Armstrong, that she wasn't fit for that yet. But she could, and did, hang up last year's paper chains, and arrange Christmas cards along the dresser.

'None from the Simons,' she remarked to Linda Burrell later in the morning. 'I wish I knew why Anne has it in for me.'

Linda didn't meet her eyes. 'The baby's crying makes Anne so tired. Then she—sort of—takes things to heart.'

'But takes *what* to heart? What am I supposed to have done?'

'I did tell you. About Cuddymoor.'

'But surely... we've been friends all our lives...'

'I dare say it'll blow over.' Linda got out her car keys. 'And you really don't need anything from town?'

'Thanks again, but you've stocked the fridge so well, I shan't have to shop till after Christmas.'

'Christmas...' Linda began.

Helen prepared to fend off the invitation she knew would be coming. In her present mood, the thought of joining the Burrells for Christmas dinner was unbearable, but how to word her refusal?

As it turned out, she didn't need to.

'We're having our turkey in the evening, this year. It's rather a nuisance, but——' Linda broke off with a hunted look. 'If you're sure there's nothing you need, I'd better be going.'

'I'm sorry you couldn't stay for coffee.' Helen took up her coat for the usual escort to the front door.

'So am I.' Linda spoke too fast. 'I'll see you when the Chris... I mean...' She floundered, and gave up. 'Soon.'

That was the trouble with convalescing, it left you far too much time to think. During work hours Helen might never have noticed her friend's odd embarrassment, but in today's emptiness it nagged away like toothache on top of appendicitis.

'And that's you, Mike Armstrong,' she told him inside her head. 'Appendicitis.'

And yet how could she talk like this, when he'd looked after her so well? Given so generously of his time and trouble, which were worth far more than mere cash?

She was still struggling with her contradictory emotions that evening, when young Robby Burrell returned Betsy.

'She's great with the sheep,' he said, with the air of one who had more to do than talk about flu. 'And she gets on a treat with old Gyp. Can I have her again tomorrow?'

'So you're helping Will out over Christmas?'

'Will's away,' Robby told her loftily. 'I'm in charge.'

'Away where?' Helen asked, intrigued to hear of this sudden departure of her quiet neighbour who hardly ever travelled.

'Not sole charge, mind. We've Dan Allen for the lambing.'

'But that must be costing Will a bomb! What on earth——?'

'Can I have Betsy again tomorrow?' Robby blew pointedly on his hands, and stamped on the tiles of the porch. 'And Christmas Day. You won't miss her, what with church and the "do" after.'

'What "do"?'

'I'm not bothering with that—too busy. Can I have . . . ?'

Helen agreed that he could, and he disappeared in Will's old Land Rover. Mixing Betsy's supper, rejoicing to have her back, Helen still couldn't help thinking about what he'd called 'church and the "do" after'. He'd taken it for granted she was invited, but she wasn't. And if he didn't know it, his mother did.

'That's why Linda was so odd this morning. What's happening to them all?' Helen set Betsy's bowl in its place. 'Will Purvis off to foreign parts, the rest of the village up to something or other on Christmas Day... Whatever next?'

The answer to that turned out to be Mike Armstrong, on the phone at about eight. 'So you did stay in.'

'This is harrassment,' Helen snapped, refusing to admit to herself how glad she was to hear his voice.

'Just making sure you haven't gone carol-singing.'

'What? You really think I'd be fool enough——'

'Ah.' The deep tones cut through hers. 'Welcome back the crabby little grouch we all know and——' He stopped, then sounded suddenly, unaccountably weary. 'If you've enough energy to be this bad-tempered, you're well again.'

'I'm...' Torn between wanting to contradict him, and the need to show her independence, Helen stammered to a halt. 'I'm fine,' she managed at last.

'Or anyway, you will be tomorrow, in time for the party.'

'The party.' She worked very hard to keep the forlorn note from her voice. 'So you were asked to that, too?'

'Everybody and their granny was asked. But don't worry, I won't be there.' A huge, cold emptiness settled in his voice. 'So that's it, then,' he added, as if this really were a final separation. 'Merry Christmas, and see you around some time.'

Only when she put the phone down did that familiar sense of loss break over her. She couldn't doubt it, he'd intended this as a final goodbye. Just one last check that she was taking proper care, not wasting all the work he'd put into looking after her, and that was that. Mission accomplished. From now on, he'd just be one of the people she saw about the village.

But how could he ever be that? How could she ever stop hating him for the ruthless business instincts which were about to destroy her beloved Cuddymoor? And how could she hate him at all, when he'd been so good to her in so many ways? And what had hatred or goodness to do with it, when her body wouldn't let her forget his hands, his lips, the great unity she had so longed for which now would never, ever happen?

Compared with this new misery, the question of the party faded to nothing. It wasn't even a toothache—more a blister on your heel, hurting only when you pressed it. Sitting with her filled hot-water bottle on her lap, talking to her mother, she quite forgot it.

'I'm fine, honestly.'

'If you say so.' Meg seemed unconvinced and, worse, unsure how to go on. 'I'll ring later,' she decided, 'when you're feeling better.'

Helen frowned. 'That means you've something to tell me.'

'Not at all.' But Meg was clearly flustered. 'Just get well enough to enjoy yourself at the Simons'.'

'So that's who it is. Now I know why——' Helen stopped, hoping she hadn't already given too much away.

'You are going?' Sure enough, Meg's sharp maternal ears had picked up more than they were meant to. 'It's the christening.'

'Little Stacey?' Helen couldn't keep the surprise and pain from her voice.

'It seems Christmas Day is also the feast of St Anastasia. You didn't even know that?'

'It's not exactly one of the ten things everybody knows about Christmas.' Helen tried, not very successfully, to keep her tone light. 'So they're having the new baby christened on her saint's day?'

'It's Anne's fancy. She's been so low, Jim went along with it, but I bet he doesn't know——' Meg's indignation grew '—that you haven't been asked. Honestly——'

'Don't go on about it, Mother. It's only a party.'

What was a party, compared to a whole dreary lifetime? What was the loss of one friendship, compared to the great emptiness of a lost... Helen gripped the phone tighter.

'I'll be in church anyway, Christmas Day.'

'All by yourself among the invited guests,' Meg fumed. 'I feel like telling that Anne Simon a thing or two.'

'Don't you dare!'

'You're ill, you're about to lose——'

Meg stopped in mid-flow, and Helen frowned. Her mother was holding something back, the same uneasy something she had earlier refused to speak about.

'About to lose what?'

'Nothing.'

'You might as well tell me.'

'So you're really feeling better?'

Helen sighed. Whatever it was, not a word would come through until Meg was good and ready to tell it. They might just as well wind up the call.

'Troubles always come in threes,' she observed to Betsy as she put the phone down. 'I'm a social outcast, I'm going to be an old maid...'

Betsy's sympathetic brown gaze went blurry, and Helen dashed the sleeve of her dressing-gown across her eyes. If she once gave way, it might never end.

'And besides those,' she managed, only a little throatier than usual, 'something else is coming my way that I don't yet know about. Oh, well.' She stood up, the hot bottle under her arm and Betsy at her heel. 'Whatever it is, it can't be worse.'

She had an uneasy feeling of tempting fate, but two worries at a time were enough to take to your lonely room. Especially when one of them was knowing that you would be lonely there for the rest of your life.

'I was right about him the first time.' She settled Betsy in her usual corner. 'He's a devil.'

But he'd slept in the rocking-chair just here, hair all up in points, face smooth as a boy's. And he'd put these freesias here on her bedside table, and you couldn't throw them out, could you, not beautiful flowers like this? Snuffling up the combined scents of freesias and nutmeg, Helen scrambled into bed and put out the light.

And that was when the pain really started. Here, in this bed, his strong arm had propped her up, his strong hand had raised that marvellous, soothing drink to her lips. And here, too, they might have taken their pleasure together. Only it wouldn't have been just pleasure, not with Mike Armstrong. What they'd almost plunged into was much deeper, much more important, though she'd scarcely understood it at the time and now never would ...

'Think of something else,' she told herself in desperation. 'Anything else. Little Stacey Simon. What a hissy sort of name. When I have babies ...'

Wrong again.

His phrase, but it fitted. She'd never have babies. She'd never have anyone, or be anything but Helen Thornton, the poor old lady alone in Thornton Pele.

Alone!

Wide-eyed, she raised herself on one elbow. Then she switched on the bedside light, and faced with absolute certainty the news her mother had refused to tell.

The clues had always been there, if she'd recognised them. Nora had known, hence all the long, confiding phone calls. And it explained the weekly lunches at Pele Farm.

'No wonder my mother wouldn't stop those.'

Helen squirmed anew. How paltry she'd been, how crass, to try and stop her mother seeing Will. Shy Will, forty-three and unmarried, quiet and reserved, yet always with a special look in his eyes when he greeted Meg.

'They've loved each other for years,' Helen realised with shame. 'I never saw it because I didn't know what love meant. Not then ... but I won't think about that.'

No, she'd think about her mother and Will. It wasn't just for Nora that Meg was staying away, it was to make Will realise how he'd miss her, and overcome his shyness. And he had, so much that he'd finally left his beloved sheep and gone to Edinburgh to propose. And Meg had accepted.

Half out of bed to telephone her congratulations, Helen glanced at the clock. 'I can't disturb her at this hour,' she decided. 'But in the morning, I have to do everything I can to stop her feeling bad about leaving me alone here.'

Alone here. Mike Armstrong had once asked her, with a hesitation rare in him, if she'd ever thought about that.

'He knew,' she realised wonderingly. 'How could he know when I didn't?'

She put the thought resolutely away, and switched off the light. She must concentrate very hard on her mother's happiness, very hard indeed ...

Maybe she succeeded, or maybe her healthy body just took the time off to cure itself. For whatever reason, she scarcely felt the duvet closing round her, and didn't wake till eight. Seeing that it was Sunday, she could ring Edinburgh at once.

'We've talked it over. Will and me, that is,' Meg added with loving pride. 'And we did wonder if you might think again about selling to Mike.'

'He won't want to buy now,' Helen said quickly.

'But he'll need somewhere, when the summer lets begin at Moor Cottage. He says——'

'Whatever he says, he won't want Thornton Pele. Any more than I'd want him to have it. And after all,' Helen rushed on, 'you're only moving down the road.'

'That's true. I'm leaving Milburn and Harkness, so I'll still be able to help you.'

'You're not even to think of it. You'll find plenty to do on the farm.'

'We are going to redecorate,' Meg admitted.

Helen asked all the right questions, made all the right noises. Only when she hung up, and looked round the great empty space, did it come to her that nothing here would ever be the same again. On this, too, Mike Armstrong had been right.

'Change happens, whether you welcome it or not.'

She could almost hear the deep voice saying it. And that other time, when her body had still been singing from his touch, and she'd told him he'd never get Thornton Pele through her.

'Noted. It can fall apart any way you want it to.'

Which, on nothing but her own strength and income, was just what it would do. Gone her hopes of ever affording good heating, a living-room above stairs, fresh paint throughout.

When she handed Betsy over to Robby Burrell, and made her solitary way back across the great hall, she knew it would never be warmed by a log fire, softened with carpets, hung with pictures as she'd so often dreamed. She'd kept Thornton Pele for the Thornton family—and a lot of good it would do her, the last of the line who would never, ever marry.

Those flats at the top of the house might have been all right, if she'd only given herself time to think. Living there separately, she and Mike Armstrong might have become friends over the years like her mother and Will. And then maybe, like her mother and Will . . . But no, they wouldn't, they wouldn't.

'How could I,' she burst out as the scent of nutmeg swirled round her, 'be friends with him after what he's said?'

But the scent only followed wherever she went. It persisted through all the soap and beeswax and turpentine, all her frenzied activity to catch up on jobs she'd had to leave during her flu.

'At least I'm over that,' she realised some time later in the morning. 'Well enough to organise my own traditional Christmas.'

Which meant something reasonably festive from the freezer. This partridge would do, she'd have it ready by tomorrow evening and eat it by candle-light the way she and Mike . . . She dumped the partridge in an oven tray, and left it to defrost.

Now for a real fire, in the little cast-iron fireplace of the sitting-corner. She set light to the paper and sticks, put up the fireguard, and went at last to fetch holly from the bush by the pele tower. She tried very hard to enjoy the ritual as she usually did, but this year she couldn't help noticing the way the leaves prickled through her gloves, and rattled in the wind as she carried the branches back to the house.

And it was cold, this wind. It made your eyes water so that you couldn't believe what you saw. He couldn't be real, this figure rising from the sleek car in the drive. He must be a noonday devil, she decided, and would have walked through him if he hadn't stopped her with a very solid grip on her arm.

'Ouch!' He let go. 'That holly's dangerous.'

She kept it between them. 'Why have you come?'

'Your mother rang me,' he told her gently. 'Last night.'

So Meg had been spreading the good news.

'She might have waited till she talked to me.' Helen said bitterly, and remembered that Mike Armstrong had probably known about it for months anyway. 'I suppose you're all ready now with your bid?'

He looked puzzled. 'That's an odd way of putting it.'

'Well, you've wasted a journey. I'm still not selling.'

'Selling? What are you on about?'

'Haven't you come here to make an offer for the house?'

'On Christmas Eve? Why the hell would I do that?'

'It must have been the first thing you thought of.' But she was beginning to be confused. 'When you heard about my mother and Will.'

'Heard what?' The question was clearly genuine. 'I know Will fancies Meg like anything, and I had an idea she might——'

'But...she must have told you they're marrying?' Helen asked, uncertain at last.

'So old Will's finally proposed?' The white, slightly irregular smile broke wide and heart-warming. 'And she's taken him? That's great!'

'But if you didn't know that,' she said carefully, 'why did you expect me to have changed my mind about selling the house?'

'You and this damned house!'

'You needn't——' She broke off with a gasp as a holly branch writhed in the wind and jabbed her cheek.

'Give me that stuff.'

He took it before she could protest. Turning the branches down out of harm's way, he lifted her hand from the scratch. She closed her eyes, the smart in her cheek forgotten in the numbing pleasure, the hopeless, never-to-be-fulfilled promise of his touch on her hand, her cheek.

'Is it still hurting?'

'No.' She drew away from him to rally her strength. 'You'd better come in.'

Once in the kitchen, he went to the sitting-corner where her fire lay exactly as she had left it.

'You don't get any better at this, do you?'

'The chimney's cold,' she snapped, indignant both with the fire for not lighting, and with him for commenting.

'So you need more of everything. Now, let's see, paper and sticks are over there, aren't they?'

And then the wretched man had reorganised the whole thing. Worse, it crackled up the chimney the minute he put a match to it. By the time she'd hung two or three holly branches on the walls, flames were licking round the logs he'd added, and he was straightening up to look round him with pleasure.

'You've certainly made the place welcoming.'

'I needed a bit of exercise.' The next spray of holly pricked her finger, and her conscience responded with a memory of all he had done for her. 'Can I . . . offer you lunch?'

'No, thanks.' Suddenly he was another person, the cold stranger who'd bidden her goodbye. 'You could talk to me for a minute, though. Seeing I've come all this way.' He took one of the rockers, and waited till she was in the other. 'The house isn't the reason I'm here.'

'No?' She couldn't help her disbelieving tone. 'So you left your family, started out into the dark . . .'

'The roads are quieter then. I'm a fool, I suppose.' His mouth set in a bitter line. 'But when your mother told me you hadn't been asked to the christening——'

'She'd no right to do that!' Helen jerked her head up, forgetting all her careful poise.

'She hoped I might think of something to help.' His eyes held hers, unreadable. 'But I can't, can I? The only one who can help is yourself, by starting to make sense over Cuddymoor.'

Released by the loved, hated name, Helen sprang to her feet. 'If I hear about that place once more——'

'Sit down, and listen.'

'I refuse to——'

'*Sit down!*'

Propelled it seemed by the very volume, she sat.

'I'm not defending Anne.' His tone quietened. 'But you must realise we all feel exactly as she does about Cuddymoor.'

'Is that why you're here? To tell me she's right?'

'Dammit, Helen, why shouldn't a few kids come here to learn about Northumberland?'

Helen blinked. 'Why shouldn't who? Do what?'

'Schoolkids from all over England. Studying the land, the history, the people and traditions.' He shrugged. 'I could understand your being against my earlier plans, for a hotel. But once I'd got the changes through——'

'Ch-changes?' she interrupted, trying to catch up.

He stared at her. 'Are you telling me you didn't know?'

'You think I'd be against a children's study centre?' The enormity of it slowly grew on her. 'A whole generation finding out how marvellous it is here?' She shot upright once more. 'No wonder Anne's treating me like an enemy. Even Linda, even old Mrs Pringle...' She whirled on him. 'How was I to know you'd changed the plans?'

For a moment, he went on staring. Then he, too, stood up, and moved away from her to the window.

'The whole village knew it.' He looked down the wind-tossed valley. 'Your mother hundreds of miles away knew it. We talked about it right here,' he turned to her, 'the night before last.'

'About your hotel.' She cast her mind back over the brief exchange. 'Which you didn't want discussed, so you shut me up.'

He surveyed her with just the beginning of that crooked, human smile. 'Surely I was more polite than that?'

'What must you all have thought of me?' She paced to the table, and whirled round. 'Why didn't any of you tell me?'

But she knew why. She wouldn't let them. She wouldn't even look at the site. Finding she couldn't stop his project, she'd stayed away from the village rather than hear of it.

'What shall I do?' She flung herself back into her chair. 'What do I say to Anne?'

'Tell her you misunderstood, of course.'

'So I'm not one kind of idiot, I'm another.'

'At least,' he didn't move, yet somehow absorbed her into that dark-brown, half-smiling gaze, 'you're an idiot who's in favour of Camp Cuddymoor.'

'Is that what you're calling it?'

'It'll please the kids.' The smile brightened. 'It was seeing you with the Simon boys that gave me the idea.'

'But that's when you told me you'd bought the land.' She recalled how he'd taunted her. 'For a hotel.'

'I wasn't giving in straight away, was I?' The devil looked out of his eyes for a moment. 'Only, when you talked about your hawthorn, and your crab-apple——'

'Don't!' She put her hands over her ears to shut him out. 'I can't bear to think of them cut down.'

'Then it's just as well they aren't.'

'That hawthorn branch was the only horse I ever had——' She broke off, and dropped her hands. 'What did you say?'

'They're to be part of the adventure playground.'

'An adventure playground,' she repeated, thrilled to think of children climbing her trees, riding her horse. 'You can get quite a gallop on that branch, if you bounce hard enough——'

'At Hotel Thornton Pele,' he interrupted from where he still stood by the window, 'we could keep real horses.'

'I won't ever sell.' She rocked furiously. 'Whoever gets Thornton Pele has to take me, too. For life.'

'That sounds very like marriage, to me.'

She stared at him, wide-eyed. 'The last time you talked about marriage, you said awful things.'

'About run-down county families?' He gave her a sideways glance. 'I was worn out, Helen.'

She stopped rocking. It was true, he'd worn himself out looking after her. And he was here now, not to buy the house, as she'd supposed, but because he'd heard of her being hurt, and wanted to be with her.

Though that seemed the last thing on his mind now. 'And not only worn out,' he reminded her with a new look in his eye, 'but seriously frustrated. Or have you forgotten what we'd just been doing?'

'No.' She looked at her scuffed brogues, the rose-patterned curtains, anywhere but at him. 'I haven't forgotten.'

Then he was over her, lifting her hands from the wooden arms of the rocker. She struggled to free herself, weakened by the heat of those mastering hands.

'What are you doing?' she demanded as he pulled her to her feet. 'Mike!' as she found herself breathlessly close to him. 'M-Mike,' as his arms crushed her. 'M-M-Mmm...'

The world had exploded. No, *she* had exploded. No, the explosion hadn't happened yet but soon would, this blending of mouths was only the start...

'Stop it!' She struggled again.

'Shall I?' His arms still circled her. 'Shall I stop?'

Keeping her close, he buried his hand in her tossing hair. She waited fearfully while he raised one fiery tress to his lips.

'Or shall I go on?' He traced the line of her jaw and neck. 'As I wanted to when I had to undress you?'

'When you what?' She jerked her head up to stare at him. 'So that's what happened when I had flu!'

He let out a breath like steam escaping. 'You brought me to boiling-point, and you don't even remember.'

She felt the blushes overwhelming her, right to her hairline, right down over her shoulders. His hand was on her breast, kindling it through the thicknesses of wool and cotton and lace. She caught her breath, almost dizzy with desire to feel these roughened, beloved, skilful hands on her flesh.

'Could you let go of me, please?'

'Give me one good reason why.'

'So I can...well...' She dared at last to meet his eyes, with a new challenge in her own. 'My cough's all gone.'

'I see.'

Slowly, dreamily, he released her and stood back, never taking his eyes off her. Slowly, dreamily, she pulled her old green sweater over her head and dropped it. Then she held her arms wide, and met his fascinated gaze. 'Unbutton my shirt?'

'Minx.' Already he'd done it, and the shirt slid off with incredible speed. 'Well, at least you proposed to me.'

'Now my bra...I did not!'

'You did. I never had a proposal before.' The bra drifted to the rug. 'And I never intend to have another, so I won't be done out of this one.'

'I only meant——'

'Did you, or did you not,' his hand paused on her waistband, 'ask me to marry you?'

'All right. *All right*,' she breathed as the fire glowed on her nakedness. 'I'm...I'm not afraid any more, Mike. Not with you.'

Much later, still before the fire, she tangled her fingers in the hair on his chest. 'Do I seem different to you now?'

'No.' He kissed her gently on the lips. 'But you are.'

'Is it always like that?'

'No, my darling.' Already his hands were playing with her again, his lips rousing sweetness wherever they touched. 'This time, I take you with me.'

And he did, through a rainbow of the senses. And presently the rainbow's gold was hers to possess, to absorb and make a part of her being. Joined as one, they glided and skimmed through glistening inner space, launched themselves as one and found together the white cascade which lowered them gently, level by gushing level, back to the everyday world.

Where her head was pillowed on his arm, his hand on her breast, her body curled against his.

'You're not cold?' He drew her closer.

'What do you think?'

'Some things,' he agreed, 'bring their own heat.'

'And two can live warmer than one. Can we keep this rug for remembrance?'

'In our bedroom,' he murmured, eyes closed. 'Up there at the top of the house...'

'The house.' She sighed, and turned her head to kiss his shoulder. 'In the last two days, I've come close to hating it at times.'

'My beloved, fiery Helen. Always one extreme or the other.'

'Oh, I couldn't ever hate it really. I mean, I belong to it, don't I?'

'Like the stones in the walls.'

She giggled. 'Is that supposed to be poetic?'

'For a builder it is. Would you rather I said, like the oak in the floors?'

'I have been a bit like that at times, haven't I?' she admitted soberly. 'So much a part of the house, I couldn't see anything else. Obsessed.'

'With this house, that's easy to understand.'

'Is it, Mike?' She sat up. 'You're sure it's me you want, and not Thornton Pele?'

'I want both. But do you think the house would be any use to me at all, without you in it?' He raised himself on one elbow, his gaze clear, firm, serious. 'I wanted you before ever I'd set eyes on Thornton Pele. From the very first minute I saw you.'

'Out on the moors, in the storm?' As the fire-light glowed on his dark, powerful nakedness, she remembered the phantom of the lightning-flash. 'Then I was right, in a way. You were after my soul.'

He nodded. 'But I was offering mine in return.'

'O-oh.' She let out a tremulous breath, convinced at last.

'It takes two to make a bargain, though.' He rose to his feet in one sinewy movement, then drew her after him to grip her shoulders and look deep into her eyes. 'Have you really accepted me, Helen? Are you really all mine?'

She looked back into the eyes she had once found so frightening. 'All yours, Mike.'

'If we should ever have to leave Thornton Pele?'

She hesitated. 'Might we really need to do that?'

'I hope not. But I suppose it could just happen, some day.'

'Then I'd go with you,' she answered, her decision made. 'Barefoot through the world.'

The tension draining from him, he laughed and scooped her into his arms. 'So how about barefoot to your freezing bathroom? That's a fair test of anybody's endurance.'

'It's a perfectly good bathroom.' She put her arms contentedly round his neck. 'Why are we going there?'

'So you can keep me warm while I shower.'

'All right. But I've got a partridge to prepare, for our Christmas dinner.'

'Yummy!' He kissed her nose. 'When are we going to sort things out with Anne Simon?'

'Plenty of time.' She sighed luxuriously as he carried her across the great arched room, then buried her hands in his hair to slow him down.

'Wait! Can you smell it?' she asked when he had paused obligingly by the table and lowered her to her feet.

'The nutmeg? Of course. Always have.'

'You never told me,' she said indignantly.

'I've got used to it. It's just ... there, like the stones in the wall. Like the oak in the floors.' He raised her left hand to his lips, to kiss the ring finger. 'Like you and me.'

**THIS JULY, HARLEQUIN OFFERS YOU
THE PERFECT SUMMER READ!**

**EMMA DARCY
EMMA GOLDRICK
PENNY JORDAN
CAROLE MORTIMER**

From top authors of Harlequin Presents comes
HARLEQUIN SUNSATIONAL, a four-stories-in-one
book with 768 pages of romantic reading.

Written by such prolific Harlequin authors as Emma Darcy,
Emma Goldrick, Penny Jordan and Carole Mortimer,
HARLEQUIN SUNSATIONAL is the perfect summer
companion to take along to the beach, cottage, on your
dream destination or just for reading at home in the warm
sunshine!

Don't miss this unique reading opportunity.

Available wherever Harlequin books are sold.

You'll flip . . . your pages won't!
Read paperbacks *hands-free* with

Book Mate • I

The perfect "mate" for all your romance paperbacks

**Traveling • Vacationing • At Work • In Bed • Studying
• Cooking • Eating**

Perfect size for all standard paperbacks, this wonderful invention makes reading a pure pleasure! Ingenious design holds paperback books OPEN and FLAT so even wind can't ruffle pages — leaves your hands free to do other things. Reinforced, wipe-clean vinyl-covered holder flexes to let you turn pages without undoing the strap . . . supports paperbacks so well, they have the strength of hardcovers!

Pages turn WITHOUT opening the strap

SEE-THROUGH STRAP

Reinforced back stays flat

Built in bookmark

BOOK MARK

BACK COVER
HOLDING STRIP

10 x 7¼ opened
Snaps closed for easy carrying, too